retreating to peace

Punam Farmah

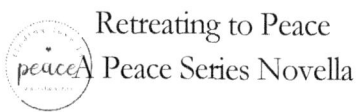 Retreating to Peace
A Peace Series Novella

Copyright © 2018 by Punam Farmah

All rights reserved as permitted under the U.S. Copyright Act of 1976. No part of this publication may be reproduced, distributed, transmitted in any form or by any means, or stored in a database or retrieval system, without the prior written permission of the author, Punam Farmah, or within the sharing guidelines at a legitimate library or bookseller.

Cover Design by Art Pratt Photography & Design
https://www.facebook.com/APphotographydesign/

ISBN Paperback: 978-1979302791

This is a work of fictions. Names, characters, places and incidents either are the product of the author's imagination or are used fictitiously, and any resemblance to any actual persons, living or dead, events or locales is entirely coincidental. The content and subject matter of this book is for those 18 years of age and older. There is strong content, violence and language.

Printed in the US.

DEDICATION

For Andrea and Boston

ACKNOWLEDGMENTS

My thanks to the fellow writers in the Peace group.
Much love and respect to Liz Mills and Kirsty Sparrow for all of their support.
A huge 'thank you' to the esteemed John Goodall for all the encouragement and advice whilst in the staff work area.
A very special acknowledgment to Ellie White, Dr. Pelham Carter, Andrea Mills and Brian Jones. Without you, there would be no Dharma. With no Dharma, there would be no Devan. You have all helped to shape my imagination and for that I am eternally grateful.

retreating to
peace

Prologue

Life can change in the blink of an eye or with the flipping of a coin. For Devan, life changed when he stuck a pin into the map that hung upon the wall of his father's study. The sharp point of the brass tack had punctured Peace, Montana. That was the name that he had seen as he opened one eye after the other, while been standing with his tongue sticking out of the corner of his mouth. Montana; he had to double check the map. Montana was all the way over there, across the pond and in the United States of America. The decision had been made and by the universe. He, Devan Coultrie, would be headed toward Peace, Montana and as soon as physically possible.

Retreating to Peace

That meant moving. Moving kit and caboodle from Rugby, England and trekking across the vast ocean. He would be leaving his family, friends and everything else that he called dear. There was after all, no reason to stay, not really. Everything was fairly messed up anyway. Death had seen to that. Death had snatched up Devan's dreams, taken a good look at them and laughed like a drain. Deaths fingers had torn up each and every one his dreams; scattering them into the four winds as though ash.

Devan had looked at the pin between his index finger and thumb as he pinched it out from the wall. It took effort to wrench it out from the brick, from against the shiny surface of the map. He would go, and to hell with the consequences.

Chapter 1

Nine months later, Devan was turning the wheel of his rather muddied Cobalt Blue Toyota and through the gates of Meadowbrook trailer park. He half smiled as he saw trailers blur through the window as he passed. In the back of his head, a vague memory played out in almost sepia tones. He had been no more than eight years old and had been taken on a family holiday to a caravan park. Devan had never thought that as an adult he would be voluntarily driving into a caravan park; his holidays had evolved since he was eight. Yet this was no holiday; this was something entirely different.

Attached to the back of the car was an RV with Colorado plates. Devan had spent the last few months there with family and friends on his mother's side. His mother had gently persuaded them to take him in, to support him during what they and his mother believed was some form of mid-life crisis. Devan had spent that time planning, prepping and battling bureaucracy. This was not a mid-life crisis, or a pipe dream, not in his head. The life that the family believed was undergoing a crisis was his. It was his life, and at thirty-four years of age, Devan could do with it whatever he wanted. He could live it how he wanted to, and no well-meaning relative would persuade him otherwise.

Devan had found the car and the trailer. All he was waiting on was the shipping container arriving in the next day or so. It had left port on the south coast of England at around the same time he had left the Midlands. Once that arrived, he would be so much happier. At the moment, his gut churned and with a combination of fear and excitement. He had heard stories, scare-stories mostly and about people emigrating. He had heard, from his extended family, about paperwork that never ended and histrionics a plenty without wanting to have any part of it himself.

Meadowbrook trailer park couldn't have been in a better position. Parking up in a spot parallel to Maple Avenue, Devan could just about see the gateway to a parcel of land not too far from the lop-sided T-junction of Oak Street. Framed by two great big strapping Oaks, the gate was the threshold to a new future, a new chapter and a whole new world. Turning the key forward in the ignition, Devan drew his foot from the clutch and heard the thunder of the engine subside. He could shrug about it now, but there had been a shed load of drama in trying to find a manual. Stick-shift and clutch were not inter-changeable; something told him that this would not be the only thing to be lost in translation.

Clambering out of the door, he placed a hand on the frame to steady himself as he took in a deep breath of cold air. Devan had stopped over in Billings to break up the drive from Colorado. A night here and night there at an assortment of trailer parks had added to the sense of adventure and heightened his growing sense of excitement. He was almost there, and his goal was in sight as he trained his gaze on the oaks in the distance. The plan was to stay at Meadowbrook for a couple of days; this would allow him the opportunity to scope out Peace. In the last few months, he had seen pictures and taken the odd virtual tour. Devan had scoured the assorted bits of paraphernalia that had been emailed and posted to him by the Realtor so that he could get a feel for the place. Passing a palm across the surface of the still warm bonnet, his focus remained on the gate and oak trees standing either side of it. Peace was picture perfect and he was ready to be part of it.

Chapter 2

"Aww," grumbled Devan as he stepped out of the rather compact shower and planted his feet onto cold linoleum. The RV was something of a sardine can in having only two berths, so the shower wasn't exactly built for sharing. "Heating, bloody hell, should have put it on," he told himself, dragging a towel from where it hung on the side of a misted up curved sliding door. Devan shivered; the hairs on his forearms were standing up on end in a feeble attempt to trap heat. Rubbing a fluffy, deep mauve towel across his limbs and torso, Devan was dripping all over the small square of linoleum that lined the bathroom. At six foot, he filled the space quite easily. To his right, was a beige colored basin;

directly opposite to it was a toilet. Bijou; when he had first looked at the RV's specs that was how the bathroom had been described.

Dropping the towel into the basin, Devan placed his feet into the clean boxers that had been dropped earlier onto floor in anticipation. The sharp and zingy scent of citrus clung to the blue and white polka dotted fabric. Whilst in Denver, his aunt-he'd forgotten which number cousin she was of his mother's-had laundered and ironed everything that she'd been able to get her hands on. Pulling up the boxers, Devan scooped up a white cotton vest to thread his arms through and tugged it on overhead. Padding out of the bathroom, he passed through into the two-berth space that went on toward the equally compact kitchen.

The rest of his clothes, a pair of dark blue turned up jeans and pale blue printed t-shirt were draped across one of the narrow beds that jutted out like shelves from the wall. Each was a very thin ledge, on the top of which sat a firm foam mattress. One of them was covered in a floral sheet and low tog duvet; that for now, was his bed. The second bed was unmade. On the ledge was a large black suitcase. Sitting on the top of the case, was a shiny black suit carrier bag. Beneath the bed were three pairs of shoes. The first of which were pair of black, highly shiny pair of brogues laced up rather tightly. Devan's second pair, were a thick soled Dr. Marten boots in oxblood; the toes had been scuffed off and away, giving them something of a battle wearied look. His third pair was a pair of heavy duty work boots with steel toe caps. He hoped to put these to work and soon.

Above the stove were heating controls and Devan tapped at the buttons to change the temperature on the thermostat. He didn't particularly fancy cooking right now; being half naked wasn't exactly conducive to it either. Placing his palms to his cheeks, he felt the coarse grain of stubble beneath his fingers.

"Shave," he said to himself, turning back towards the bathroom. "Shave, real estate office and food," muttered Devan, plotting what he wanted to do. "Have half a plan there. I can check things out; find the one horse that proverbially lives here."

Rummaging in the small cupboard below the sink, Devan located his shaving kit. Housed in the bag was a green tube of Palm Olive and a razor. Reaching in, he retrieved both and set them down behind the tap. The razor had something of a sentimental story behind it. Once upon time, the razor had belonged to his grandfather; Devan had inherited it as a gift on his 21st birthday. A curious gift, but a bequest made by his maternal grandfather who cared not for the straggly haired beards that Devan had attempted to grow in the throes of being a gawky adolescent. Made from brass, the cylindrical handle had three ridges at the base and had to be screwed into the two-inch panels that held the blade. Compared to modern razors, it was weighty and felt purposeful in his grasp. Leaving a soft haired, taupe bristled shaving brush in the bag, he put the kit aside.

Squeezing the end of the tube, Devan looked at his reflection in the circular mirror that hung on the wall. He could just about see his face as the mirror started to demist. As he lathered up the cream and rubbed it in circles across the apples of his cheeks, his reflection became less blurry. Using his fingers, he dragged the pale green cream across his cheekbones and his jaws whilst avoiding the hollows of his eyes. Jutting his chin upward, he pressed the tube again and this time applied cream to his throat. In his reflection, Devan's mouth had turned downwards at the corners. As his lips parted, his teeth were exposed and flashed in the mirror as the harsh light coming from the ceiling hit the enamel. There was an almost lupine quality to his expression as his canines were momentarily visible.

With his chin still jutting out and up, Devan put his hand to the razor and held it at his jugular. "Should have had a haircut," he said out aloud. "Make a good impression and all that."

As he dragged the razor upward towards his jaw, he exposed the scar that snaked down his throat and toward his collar bone. Thankfully, quick and effective surgery had left a fairly neat, unraised scar that according to his sister put a hefty deposit in the 'bad-ass bank'. To this day, Devan had no regrets about chasing off a would-be carjacker whilst armed with a crowbar. Armed with a homemade shank, his attacker had been as high as a kite and rather fancied his chances. All that he remembered was swinging the crow bar and then waking up in the ICU of Coventry's Walsgrave Hospital. It was an altogether unpleasant memory from a decade ago, and a lot had happened since then.

Switching the razor from one side to the other, Devan moved his gaze towards his hairline. At the center was a widow's peak from which his dark locks cascaded down his crown and landed just below his ears. He wore a relatively sleek mop of black brown locks that were only just starting to glisten in places with silver. Silver, and not grey. As far has he was concerned, silver was far more palatable than going grey. His long hair had been another area of his toilette that Devan and his grandfather had almost violently disagreed upon. Devan could not think of anything worse than a short back and sides. For now, the hair could stay. As he moved his head a little to the side, droplets of water escaped from his hair and landed on his shoulder where they glistened. Tutting sharply, he picked up the towel that had been dumped earlier and rubbed his thin but bountiful locks dry. Tossing away the now very wet towel, Devan resumed shaving and quickly got rid of the stubble. On his arms, there were goose pimples still. He remained half-dressed and the RV's heating was struggling to get to the bathroom.

Seven and a half minutes later, Devan was free of stubble and wiped away the odd splodge of shaving cream that remained. He pulled out a small tube of cocoa butter from his shaving kit and dotted some across his face. Devan pulled a face as he rubbed in the moisturizer. The stinging sensation against freshly shaved skin was why he didn't do this very often. Devan would grit his teeth and bear it as he rubbed it in; wrinkles could wait and for as long as possible.

Rinsing the razor, he returned it to the bag along with everything else. Only a little warmer than before, Devan made his way back to his bedroom and saw to getting dressed. As he pulled on socks, his jeans and t-shirt, a list formed in his head. "I need feeding," he told himself; he could feel hunger starting to throb in his stomach and hear the grumbles as it grew. "Groceries too, there was that Brightman's place," Devan said, letting out a deep sigh and running a hand through his hair. As absent-minded as it was, his fingers tugged out tangles that made him wince. "Do that first," Devan continued. "Then really face Peace. Pick up my keys," he said with a confident nod and catching his reflection in the window. "You've waited months, dear heart. What's another twenty-four hours?"

Chapter 3

Zucchini. His courgette was Montana's zucchini. Devan had chuckled quietly to himself as he shopped in Brightman's. There wasn't an awful lot that a bachelor living in a caravan might need. He was going to have lunch in the diner, but still needed to stock up the small fridge in the RV. A boy still had to eat, and not always in the local diner. Picking up two shiny green-black courgettes, Devan dumped them next to the red and yellow sweet peppers that already sat in the handbasket that dangled from his wrist. He had half a recipe in his head; the vegetables could be thrown into tomato sauce that could then envelope fresh fusilli that also been found. Devan was taking his time; deliberately so, to mooch around the store. His oxblood Dr. Martens shuffled softly across the floor that in the harsh light of fluorescent strip lighting was covered in the tracks of trolleys. This was his local supermarket, so it paid to scope the place out.

"Hi," he said softly and with a nod, as he passed a red-haired woman. She was tending to a strawberry-blonde child who sat in the trolley and swung dimpled legs against it.

"Hey!" came the reply as he passed, and the woman nodded back.

Devan grinned, his worn-down canines momentarily visible as he waved at the child and moved on. Looking over his shoulder, he caught the child waving back and with chubby digits splayed out wide. He found himself standing in an aisle of canned and jarred goods; Devan was after tomatoes. A simple Ragu wouldn't break the bank and would be fairly simple to cook up. Curling his fingers around two cans, he picked them up and dropped them into his basket. As he turned, he saw that the mum and child were not too far away at the top of the aisle. As the woman arranged her groceries, Devan saw that he was being eyeballed by the child. A little girl most likely, he thought, dressed in a pink pinafore dress with grey tights. She had by far the brightest blue eyes that Devan had ever seen and the roundest of pudding faces. Her two front teeth were only just visible between two pink, fleshy lips that formed from a cupid's bow. She was waving at him again, and laughing. Dropping the jars, Devan laughed too and waved back in return.

Children, mop haired and chubby cheeked. He remembered talking to her about children. Devan wanted at least two, but there was no way, no how he was ever going to father a whole football team. Children had definitely been part of the plan; their plan. She had been the only woman that he wanted to have a life with, to have babies with. Mop haired, chubby cheeked, and didn't inherit his slightly too big for his face, almost Roman nose.

That had been the plan. Then came the car crash; the plans had been smashed to smithereens and ground into tarmac.

Devan felt his face flush. The vapid grin that had bloomed across his face faded just as the little girl had turned her face away. A whole universe-or the chances of one-had collided with a supermarket Heavy Goods Vehicle and been destroyed in seconds. Devan registered the weight of the basket upon his arm, not to mention the hot tears starting to well up in his eyes. Sniffling loudly, he coughed away tears and turned on his heel to the check out. He needed a stiff drink-at this hour it would have to be tea-there was a box of tea bags and half fat milk nestled in the hand basket. The tea would come later, for now he was hungry. For now, he'd pay for his groceries and then head to the diner to be fed, to scope it out. Today was all about prepping for Peace; prepping to be a part of it.

Chapter 4

He had changed his mind. Devan wanted the keys to his patch of Peace as soon as he possibly could. Having visited Brightman's, he returned to the RV at Meadowbrook to dump his groceries. Standing in the middle of the caravan, Devan looked at his would-be evil twin in the narrow mirror riveted into the wall. Stepping back to see the whole of himself and not just his torso, Devan stood with his feet a shoulder width apart and his arms crossed. Clad in clean royal blue socks, his size ten feet looked less like canoes. His boxers were still clean and crisp as he buttoned up a powder blue shirt that like the rest of his wardrobe had been ironed by his aunt to within an each of its life.

Leaving his top button undone picked up a pair of navy blue trousers would ordinarily have been part of a three-piece suit. The other two thirds were still in the bag that rested atop a suitcase.

One by one, Devan slowly threaded his legs into the trousers and pulled them up. He heard a squeaky pop from his left leg as the kneecap moved and groaned in protest. This was a kneecap that proudly wore a scar from having undergone surgery. A mistimed tackle and sharp studs was always going to be something of a lethal combination. Tucking his shirt into the waistband, Devan zipped up his fly and smoothed the shirt down his stomach. For now, middle age was at bay, but a gentle curve was starting to form in not having played football for quite a few months. Football; here that would be soccer. It would always be football to him; perhaps he could bring it to town. That would be his contribution to Peace as a new resident.

Planting his hands firmly on his hips, Devan stuck out his lips in something of a pout. "A state full of cowboys, but one remains an English gentleman," his lips relaxed into a smirk. "Food." Speaking out aloud did make him feel a bit odd. But for now, he was keeping his own company. "And keys," he shuffled toward the vacant bed and his black brogues. He should have worn brown ones, but had yet to buy a pair. Sliding his feet in, Devan tied the laces. He had worn the shoe on a

Retreating to Peace

handful of occasions, yet the leather was still to relax and wrinkle. This made the shoes feel altogether heavy on his feet. Grabbing his jacket from the suit carrier, he also put his hands to a chocolate colored satchel that he slung over a shoulder. Leaving the caravan and then the park, Devan went on foot to turn right down Oak Street and left onto Main Street. Rifling through his satchel, he took out a glossy map of Peace. Standing at the cross roads, he looked from the map and down the street.

"All right, Sheila," Devan said with a quiet chuckle. "I'm coming to get you."

Chapter 5

Toffee and sesame; as Devan took a mouthful of black coffee, he savored the sweet toffee flavor that was tinged with slightly bitter, burned sesame. There was a distinct potency to the coffee, and Devan pulled a face as he set the white coffee cup down into liquid that formed a puddle in the middle of the matching saucer. By birth, Devan was a tea drinker. However, the odd cup of black coffee with at least three teaspoons of sugar stirred into it was never going to hurt. With his coffee in top left of the setting at the gingham covered table, Devan poured over a legal pad that was sat in front of him and at a slight angle. On the lined leaf was a list, at the top of which were the words 'Keys' and 'Realty peace'. These were followed by 'shipping container', 'utilities' and lastly, 'Farm house'.

Beneath the items was an uncapped fountain pen, paused before further items could be added. With its silver chrome barrel, the nib glinted in the sunlight that streamed into the diner. Engraved across the barrel in neat copperplate script was his full name. Devan Raaj Coultrie. The pen had been a gift on his thirtieth birthday from his friend Aditi. She had put a lot of thought into it; going as far as dragging him to a specialist pen shop so that he might choose one that he liked before presenting it to him. She was only the one, who knew his middle name and how to spell it correctly.

Picking up the pen with his left hand, Devan wiped away crumbs from the page with his right. Sitting not too far away was a blue and white dinner plate, cutlery and the remnants of a bacon sandwich. Devan hated crusts, and these were all that remained of his food. With his pen, he drew an arrow from the list to add additional items. "Farm house," he said quietly. "One hell of a job there, dear heart."

"Top off?" A voice to his left interrupted Devan's thoughts, as did the smudge of a coffee pot in the corner of his eye.

He looked up to his left to face the owner of the voice with his pen his hand curled above his near empty cup.

"Please," he replied, moving his arm to draw his pen toward him. "Thank you," said Devan, his eyes falling onto the name tag that identified the brown curly haired waitress. "Laura. Not to full though; three quarters, if you don't mind."

"Three quarters," nodded Laura, smiling as she poured from the coffee pot that had been just out of his blind spot. "Enjoy," she added before leaving.

"Will do, thanks again," he all but called out as she walked away. Devan returned to his list and studied it further. "Builders, need to find builders and an architect too," he said with a sigh. "Once I've assessed the damage. How much could this flaming well cost me?"

Devan sat for a while, checking over his list and letting his lunch settle. He even had some pancakes, as a second course. These were smothered in syrup so as to settle his nerves before picking up his keys from the Realtors. Having finished the second cup of coffee, the legal pad was returned to his satchel. He had slung his jacket over it and removed crisp dollars from his wallet. Dollars, they felt so different compared to the pounds and pence that he was used to. Devan settled his bill and said a softly spoken goodbye to Laura behind the register.

Turning right out of the diner, Devan crossed the road to head to Peace Realty. He felt a tight knot of anxiety form in the pit of his stomach as he walked down Main Street. There was a lot riding on this; money, time, and effort had been ploughed into retreating to Peace. Most of his savings had been ploughed into purchasing Oakview and taking it over from the previous owners. Whoever the Harrington's were, the mere mention of the name had people looking a bit wary. Month of negotiations, codicils and carefully crafted platitudes had led Devan to this point. His savings had secured the land, the farmhouse and the clutch of outbuildings that sat on the one-hundred-acre parcel of land. The starts had aligned perfectly with the contents of his bank balance to ensure that there was no mortgage involved. His severance package from the bank was now earmarked to get everything up and running.

Most of his peers would shudder at the thought of stocks, savings and nest eggs. In their minds, if you had it, spend it; you could not take it with you as no shroud came with pockets. He attributed his financial savviness to his Indian and part Scottish lineage. It had been drilled into him from an early age that it was important to save for rainy day. The same had been said to his siblings. Devan's sister had been encouraged to save for her wedding; if she wanted a big, Bollywood, frou-frou wedding, she would need to look after pennies so that the pound could look after themselves.

Arriving at Peace Realty, Devan paused outside a moment and drew in a deep breath. Retreating to Peace was not something that he had thought about lightly. This was a new chapter, a new start. This was jam making in Montana, a fantasy that he and Carly had from time to time joked about. Steeling himself, he gulped down his fears and went in.

Half an hour later, a clutch of keys sat nestled in his pocket and a neatly word-processed title deed was tucked into his satchel. It had taken all of ten minutes to sign the deeds, take up ownership when it had taken him years to save up and all his pennies. Oakview was all his. Signed, sealed and he was the owner occupant of the property and the whole parcel of land that it sat upon. The plot of land was a brand-new universe to be played with and on his terms.

"Thank you, Kiki," he had said, recapping his fountain pen and sliding it into his satchel. "I promise to look after it all," he had held out his hand, and to have it shaken by the blonde haired, beautifully buoyant woman who ran the agency. "Englishman's home and all that. Oakview is now my castle, my home and my manor. You can tell that to the Harrington's and then some."

Kiki gave something of a wicked laugh and shook his hand. "You're welcome, Devan," she said, her eyes twinkling somewhat. It did feel as though she was listening and closely to his accent. Whilst it wasn't the

Queen's English, there can't have been much flattened out English floating around Montana.

"I'll see you, Kiki," said Devan putting on his jacket, there had been something of a nip in the air as he had walked here. "Thanks again."

Devan took his time meandering down Main Street with his hands tucked into his pocket. The newly acquired keys jangled and jostled in the lining against his leg. His mind whirred with potential plans and items that he could to add to his list of things to sort. As well as planning, he collated a mental inventory of all the shop fronts; this was after all, his locale. It would be useful to pay attention to all that filled his new home, especially if he planned to stay here indefinitely. Slowly perambulating off into Oak Street, Devan caught sight of the sturdy iron gate that he surveyed from a distance. It was flecked with paint, spotted with rust in places and flanked by two strapping oaks. The sight of the entrance rather made Devan's heart quicken and his throat tighten in anticipation. Removing his hands from his pockets, he curled his fingers around leaves forged from iron and looked at the vastness beyond. Not too far down the track, he could see the tumble-down farmhouse in all of its three dimensions. What Devan saw before him, was stark contrast to the flat computer drawn plans and agent pictures that he had seen; plans and pictures that had been distinctly lacking heart and soul.

Oakview was his; entirely his, and a chance to start again.

Chapter 6

March had gently segued to spring. By April and May, the oaks that stood sentry at the gate had gone into bud. Soon, they were crowned by lush dark green leaves and no longer looked scary or skeletal. Devan had spent the last few months trying to get the lay of the land and settling in. It would be June before he made any attempt to rescue the farmhouse and the outbuildings. His caravan, named Great Aunt Claudie, sat parked at the mid-way point between the gate and the farmhouse. Great Aunt Claudie was a fond memory from his childhood. Devan was convinced that everyone had a doddery spinster aunt, who was a little batty and had likely been around since the stone-age. Naming his RV after her was something to keep him sane as he tried to make sense of everything. He stood at the door of the caravan with a shiny white mug of tea in one hand, and a bacon sandwich in the other. Devan watched the sunrise over Peace and felt a wonderful, soul warming sense of contentment.

He had been awake for about forty minutes and the watch on his wrist had just ticked at a quarter passed six. Three yards away from Great Aunt Claudie and to his left, was his cobalt blue Toyota. The few parts of it that weren't covered in mud, shone with early morning dew. On his right and looking very much like an eyesore against yellow-green grass was a red shipping container. Contained within was Devan's whole world. Minus his 'fridge, the freezer and his well and truly knackered washing machine, his entire flat on the Hillmorton Road in Rugby had been consigned within to be transported all the way over to Peace. At this moment in time, Devan was still residing in Great Aunt Claudie.

Further down the track, the old Oakview Farmhouse was shrouded by sea-green plastic and being held up by scaffolding boards and poles. Deemed unfit for inhabitation and requiring significant Remodeling, the farmhouse didn't look particularly pretty but was pregnant with potential. Devan sipped his tea and nibbled at his sandwich. Stretching out before him was a neatly segmented half acre of land. Portioned off into eight compact beds, the half-acre was ready to be planted up with fruit and vegetables. Just by the gate was a poly tunnel; a metal framed, domed structure covered with plastic that bustled with plants. Tomatoes, pepper and squashes were all waiting to be moved out and into dirt. His study of his patch of Peace had not been entirely wasted. Devan had called his grandmother and sought her advice. As a child, he had played bare-foot amongst rows of spinach sown in her back garden. Devan remembered pulling radishes and then blaming magpies for their absence when she had gone to pick them. He also planned to sink some raspberry canes. Devan would have argued with you all day long; if you wanted proper raspberries, then you needed those that were Scottish in origin. These were currently on his wish-list, and needed to be hunted down from someplace.

He was watching cars travel down Oak Street when he heard a buzzing sound behind him. Polishing off the half a sandwich that he held on to, Devan wiped his greasy hand down his jeans to pick up his phone. He had idly left it aside on the worktop whilst brewing his tea and since it didn't ring often, didn't need it attached to his hip. Sliding his finger across the screen, Devan didn't so much as glance at the Caller ID.

"Oh my God, did I wake you?" A breathy and anxious sounding female voice tickled his senses as he pressed the device to his ear. "Devan? This is you, isn't it?" uttered the voice. "You haven't called. All you had to do was call."

He listened, trying desperately hard to locate the name of the familiar sounding voice. "Aditi?" he asked, his eyes widening as he realized. Realized exactly who it was, and then had the anxious brittleness in her voice smack him between the eyes. Devan could almost imagine Aditi standing with her palm pressed to her head in the throes of sheer drama, with her eyes wide with fright; even wider than usual. He could feel his lips twitch and slide into a smile. Aditi had such big, beautiful, almond shaped eyes; framed by the longest eyelashes that he had ever seen. Eyes that somehow made her look permanently scared. Except for when she would smile; Aditi's eyes would light up and flicker with the promise of passion, peril and pure ecstasy.

"Devan? Devan, are you there?" Aditi gasped softly, drawing breath in nervous anticipation. "I couldn't remember the time difference between here and there."

His daydream was momentarily broken, and Devan quickly glanced at his watch. "Yes. Yes, I'm here," replied Devan, trying to calm himself. Aditi had set his heart racing; he didn't expect her to call, to hear her voice. Taking a gulp of tea, Devan calmed himself. "I'm awake, just about. My God, Aditi, you sound awful," he was only lying in part. "What's the matter, you okay?" he asked, knowing that if she were here, he would probably throw his arms around her.

"Devan," whispered Aditi, the sound of his name strained between sobs and gulps. "Devan, you ran off. Ran off and I bloody well miss you."

"I miss you too," he said softly. His heart thudded loudly. Devan felt his ribs twinge as though he had been elbowed sharply. "Hold on. I'm putting you on loud speaker. I also need some more tea," he added removing the 'phone from his ear and leaning against a jar of Raspberry jelly. It had been a lucky find in Brightman's but had failed to make it to his breakfast when the bacon had called his name from the fridge. As the kettle still had some water in it, he flicked it on and leant against a worktop with his arms crossed.

"Like hell you miss me!" spat out Aditi. Given the ferocity of her tone, she may as well have been standing there in front of him and not several thousand miles away. "You ran off," she repeated; her words were still seething through sobs and sniffles. "No thought to anyone else, those you've left behind. And now, now when I need you…when Chris is being an arse…." Aditi sniffed loudly and over the sound a tissue being rustled.

The name hit a nerve, several. "Chris?" he asked, his tone rising as he stood up a little straighter. His nerves pinged as he said it, his hackles were raised full hoist. "The hell are you still with him, Aditi?" he asked shrilly as the kettle boiled. "Time and time again, you get sucked in. He promises you the world, and then KABOOM!" he said waving his hands around wildly, before curling his fist and shaking it at the window. "What did he do this time?" ventured Devan, picking up his half a cup of tea and draining it away down the sink. "Cancelled a weekend away, had a pow wow with his ex-wife? His daughter called you a-" he broke off and bit his tongue. Devan could hear Aditi cry, her tears crackled across the line to a different continent. Pouring water into his mug, he put the kettle back onto its base.

"Just listen would you," uttered Aditi, inhaling sharply. "He said it's over, and that he's not ready to start again. And you…you ran off. Chris is cutting me loose; I'm alone, and without you. You swanned off; you swanned off to sulk and in a different country. How is that fair? How am I supposed to get through this and without the one person that I thought I could rely on? I need you; tell me what to do, Devan."

He put his hand to a jar labelled tea, unscrewed the lid and fished out a circular tea bag. "Aditi," he said, keeping his tone level, and trying to be gentle. "You are a grown up. Yes, Chris is a bona fide crap hole. You deserve better, you know that," he couldn't help but shake his head as he dropped the tea bag into hot water. "I've told you this before, and so many times. Personally, I would knee cap him," said Devan, curling his lips in disdain. "Maybe even break up the rest of him and throw him into the Avon."

There was a brief moment of silence between them, before Aditi started to laugh. Her vulnerability and the distance between them made him feel more than a little uneasy.

"Aditi, I've known you since we were kids," he said out aloud. "Our mums worked together, for crying out loud. You've been a part of my world for longer than I can remember. I can hear your hurt, I can bloody well feel it too. But I am here, yes, thousands of chuffing miles away," he said with a shallow sigh. "So I am unable to throw the bloody cretin out of the nearest window and under a bus." Once more, he let the silence cling to the walls of the compact kitchen.

"Aditi?" he could feel the rise and fall of her name in his voice.

"Yes." It took a moment for her to reply; she had been listening, hanging onto his words. Something was hanging in the air, with the miles between them and holding them together.

"You deserve so much more," said Devan, watching his tea brew. "Chris is a horse's behind. He promises you the world, only to turn it on its head. How many more times, dear girl, do we need to talk about this? Even Carly, Carly told you! She told you, that he wasn't worth it." Looking at his mug, he figured the tea was done and was about to drink it black

"Carly!" snapped Aditi. "Carly, bloody, Carly! She's the one that took you away. You ran, because you couldn't cope. You ran because…. was bad enough, that the wretched woman came between us in the first place." Aditi's sobs had subsided, and the only drip now was that of vitriol.

"ENOUGH!" Roared Devan, it was his turn to yell; his rage bounced against Great Aunt Claudie's tinny walls. "STOP!" He growled, "Stop right there. Don't you dare talk about her like that, don't you flaming well dare." Devan slammed down his mug, vibrating with white fury. Then there were the shades of purple grief that tinged it, and made his face flash as he fumed. "I loved Carly, and she was never between us. You and I have known each other a lifetime; just think of all the stuff that has happened."

"Christmas, Devan, you've clearly forgotten." Aditi dove in sharply "The pouting all of the time and drama when visiting family. Not wanting to come to my birthday; deigns to come and then complained about it all. Carly sat there with a face like a smacked backside. She would be sniping; God, her neurotic backbiting when you weren't listening about your parents. I tried to bite my tongue, tried to be nice and for you. She died, and you escaped her clutches."

Retreating to Peace

That stuck him like an arrowhead and wham! Devan had been smacked straight in the chest. Picking up the 'phone, he hung up on Aditi and then launched the device toward the bathroom. Thudding against shower, it landed with a clunk into the floor.

Feeling bile rise in this throat, he was both stung and stunned. Never in a million years had he thought that Aditi might say such things. Devan had loved Carly; and Aditi, she meant the world to him. But her words had hurt; her words had winded him heavily. With the day only just kicking off, it was way too early for bourbon.

Chapter 7

June 16th. That was the next time that Devan heard from Aditi. He had spent eleven days distracted, in a mood best described as grey, grainy and grotesquely miserable. No part of him had realized just how much venom Aditi had been harboring for Carly. He was in the diner and making his way through a slab of meatloaf. Devan remained undecided as to whether or not he wanted to make an attempt on the puddle of peas and cache of carrots that accompanied it. Devan's 'phone was propped up against a bottle of mustard; the device vibrated and caught his attention. It had been positioned there as he was expecting a call from his mother. It had taken time, but they had forged an agreement. On a

Friday, he would sit in the diner; she would call and they would talk.

Avni could then tell the whole world that her son was okay; that contrary to popular belief, he had not gone off the rails and wasn't lying in a ditch someplace with a needle stuck in his arm. It was always Friday for him due to the time difference; his mum would get up early Saturday morning, speak with him and then take the dog for a walk.

A copy of the *Peace Herald* sat next to Devan's plate; he had been reading as he ate so as to pass the time. Pushing the paper aside, he slid an index finger across the screen of his 'phone before sitting back and clutching cutlery.

Aditi appeared on screen before him. Her lashes batted and the device did not do justice to her features. Doe-like eyes glimmered; she smiled, and her cheeks dimpled. He knew full well that Aditi had cheekbones that a supermodel would sell a kidney to have. What Devan had never noticed before, was how her lips would purse before she spoke. Purse and pucker, as though he needed to will her to utter something. Tilting his head, he studied smudges of mascara that framed her eyes, and the tinge of fading red lipstick that stained her cupid's bow shaped lips.

"Meatloaf again?" asked Aditi, her lips parting into a smile and exposing shiny, square, flashy white teeth. "I spoke to Avni. Apparently, Friday night is meatloaf and misery," she giggled before rolling her eyes slowly. "Perhaps I could help get rid of the misery for you. Don't worry, this is not a booty call and from all the way over here."

Holding a knife and fork, Devan squinted at the image. "You've not gone to bed yet, have you?" he asked, skewering a stack of carrots with his fork. "I'm still cheesed off with you, Aditi. Do you really want to rattle my cage and when you're not exactly match fit?" he continued, arching his brow and dropping carrots into his mouth.

Closing her eyes, Aditi took in a deep breath through her nose. It caused her nostrils to twitch. With a nose like hers that slightly turned up at the end, there was an added air of haughtiness to her. "I know," she said opening her eyes, and letting her eyelashes unfurl and fan out. "I'm sorry," whispered Aditi. "I shouldn't have said what I said. I didn't mean to hurt you, Devan. I love you; you mean the world to me. I hate it when we fight." Her eyes were glimmering, and the smallest of tears were starting to travel.

About to cut up more meatloaf, Devan felt his gaze be pulled from the peas on his plate and toward Aditi's pout. There was something about her words, the sadness that edged them; there was a twinge in his gut that she pulled at figuratively with her fingertips. She was also in tears, and that always swung a lead across his chest. "We shouldn't fight then, should we," he replied, unable to suppress an almost lupine smile. "I love you too, Aditi. Known you forever, why would I change that? Besides, I'm not running, you are."

"I am?" asked Aditi, her face flushing a little and her brow creasing. Pink and an olive Asian skin to never matched well, not even with the black-blue eyeliner that now rather dramatically ringed her eyes.

"Eyeliner," Devan laughed deeply, as he tapped his eye. What he wanted to do was to reach forwards and wipe it away. "Or did Chris do something again? Calling up strange men and in the wee hours; you sure that this isn't a booty call?" Devan could be wry; he and Chris tended to look at each other with grating discomfort.

Aditi pressed her fingers across the hollows of her eyes and then looked at them to see the damage. "We both know what happened, when there was an actual booty call," she had started to smirk, and bit her lip as she arched a brow. "And you wonder why you and Chris aren't friend," added Aditi, waggling a finger. "You and I have history, or don't *you* remember, Devan?"

Clearing his throat, Devan looked around a little nervously. "Shh," he urged, leaning forward a little. "History that we don't talk about; don't you remember? Miss. My heels hurt, can't walk in a straight line, will you carry me."

The memory had been hazy, but at the mere mention had become fully blown and salient in his mind. He'd been a perfect gentleman at the time and even said no, several times and in different languages to carrying her. To this day, he couldn't look at spike heels in the same way again. It had been the whole falling over the cat, landing in her arms and not being able to find his boxers the next morning that had complicated things.

"Okay, okay, okay," laughed Aditi; she could laugh like a drain and then some, but pressed a digit to her lips. Her eyes darted to the right as there was the sound of a door creaking open. "I have to go," she said, kissing the tips of her fingers and blowing the kiss to him. "Call your mum at tea time. I called you, so that she could have a lie in. Love-" Aditi paused as a shadow loomed over her. "Bye, Devan," she waved and promptly hung up.

"Bu-" Devan was cut off by his 'phone changing its screen. He knew who had caused the shadow and for it to loom over Aditi. It was a shadow that he would have taken great pleasure by kicking into touch. That was however a little difficult when he was so far away from Aditi; it was also a painful reminder of all that he had left behind. Letting out a deep breath, he saw his own nostrils flare as a reflection on the 'phone screen.

"You do deserve better," he muttered under his breath. As he cut up more meatloaf, his mind whirred with how he might hypothetically bump off Chris. Sat here, thousands of miles away in Peace, all that he could do was imagine kneecapping the poor excuse for a human being that his best friend desperately clung onto for a happily ever after. This would all stay in his head, he couldn't and wouldn't tell Aditi. In his head, there was no harm, no foul. No one got to hurt Aditi, not if he could help it.

Chapter 8

Rumor had it, that this was meant to be a big weekend. More specifically, it was Founder's week and when Peace would come alive with a carnival atmosphere. The date was now the 20th of July and Devan had been awake since about seven in the morning. During the week, there had been all sorts of anticipatory talk in the diner. He had popped into Toppin's the previous night and had heard all about bonfires and rodeo grounds, plus the concert that was scheduled. Devan had crawled out of his bed and walked to the diner clutching a thermos-mug.

Saturdays were his one day to be lazy, and a breakfast of syrupy pancakes with hot coffee was now very much part of his routine. He had loitered at the diner for a while; and it was half past nine by the time that he had finished eating and asked for his mug to be filled with half a liter of black coffee. From what he understood, the parade would begin at ten; so he had ventured into town early to secure a vantage point. Pouring a couple of teaspoons of sugar into his coffee, Devan stirred it with a knife as he stood by the counter. Coffee and sugar were altogether necessary at that moment in time. The one beer at Toppin's had become about three or four, after which the karaoke that drifted around didn't assault his senses so much. Screwing the lid onto his mug, Devan took a mouthful to make sure of the sweetness. "Mmm, that will do," he said quietly.

"Laura, I will see you!" As he left, he waved at the waitress who was taking orders at the other end of the diner. As his Saturday breakfast routine had become established, he had been waited upon by Laura and most of the time. "Enjoy the weekend, don't eat too much cotton candy now will you. See you in the week."

"Bye, Devan, you too!" replied Laura, briefly looking up from her pad and waving back.

Exiting Sheila's, Devan removed a pair of sunglasses that had been tucked into the collar of his pale blue linen shirt. Unfolding the arms with his one hand, he then threaded them on to his ears and toward his nose. He couldn't remember the last time that it rained, but in reality, he really didn't care. British by birth, he had seen enough rain to last for a life time and didn't want to see anymore anytime soon. The distinct lack of precipitation meant that all of his winter woollies-heavy jumpers, long coats and such like-were still stowed away in the bowels of the shipping container sitting by car. His clothes could stay there a while; he would worry about winter in Montana later. He travelled towards the B&B and located a spot to stand, to watch and immerse himself in the color and culture of Peace.

There was a full day of celebrations ahead of him. Devan rather fancied checking out the culinary contests involving chili, corn bread and barbecues. He'd have a good mooch; least of all because the end products were all edible and he wouldn't be the one washing up at the end of the evening. Later, he fancied trekking up to the rodeo ground, seeing if there was a bonfire. The only bonfires he knew of were the ones lit to celebrate Guy Fawkes and Parliament not going up in flames. Swigging his coffee, Devan stepped back towards the doors of the B&B and braced as a throng of people filled the street. Some part of him felt at peace and he rather liked it. He also liked barbecue, but that was a different ball game altogether.

Chapter 9

Bleary eyed, Devan bumbled around his rather compact bedroom as he dressed in the dark. He was convinced that Great Aunt Claudie was spinning and that with every step that he took, his body throbbed. His stomach lurched over and over as he pulled on a clean t-shirt and a pair of dark jeans. For the moment, he had no idea how he had returned home. As he stepped into the kitchen, Devan caught sight of a beige Stetson dangling off the back of a chair. On the worktop next to the stove were two toffee apples, one of which was still in its cellophane wrapper. The other was half eaten; the otherwise crisp white flesh had started to turn an interesting shade of brown with exposure to air. Devan had been about to reach for the kettle, he was desperately in need of a good, strong, cup of tea. Only his stomach was in severe and pained disagreement; the sensation was so intense he was compelled to turn on his heel and head straight to the bathroom.

Only just making it, he held the toilet bowl in his arms as though he was greeting a long-lost friend. He was there a while, as his stomach emptied itself of beer, barbecue and acrid mess of yellow acid. Such were the consequences of over indulgence, of enjoying the carnival atmosphere and a little too much.

With his stomach feeling lighter and no sensation of being on a spin cycle to the point of being disorientated, Devan tried to make tea again. Leaning heavily against the worktop with his digits splayed out across the surface, he was still feeling more than a little discombobulated. It was taking a supreme effort to stay upright and not fall to the floor into a Devan-shaped puddle. His plan for today had been to hit Main Street again. After the parade and the bonfire yesterday, there was fair scheduled. Turning over his right wrist, he peered at his watch. "Half eleven, bloody hell," he muttered. "Must have been hammered half way to hell," he told himself. "God only knows what happened," he tried to think; shaking his head, the pain told him no.

Hearing the kettle boil, he slowly but steadily set about making tea. It was then that he saw his 'phone resting against the toaster, then there was the bright pink boa sat next to it and with its end snaking towards the floor. Putting his one hand to the boa, he draped it around his neck and threw one end over his shoulder with a flourish. With the other hand, he scooped up his 'phone. There were over two dozen missed calls and messages; they were all from the same person. He had to blink and focus himself as he doubled checked the name. He was starting to sober up a little as the 'phone vibrated, and the name of the caller flashed up on screen.

"Open your door, Devan," said the voice. "It's hot, I'm tired, and God only knows what we're missing in town."

Devon dropped his 'phone to the floor, bounded across the RV and opened the door. There stood before him, was the incessant caller and owner of the voice.

"Hello, Gorgeous," said Aditi, giggling and with menace. "How's your head this morning?"

Chapter 10

"I don't remember a single solitary thing," stated Devan as he picked up a white coffee mug. He pressed the rim to his lips and drew in a hearty mouthful of heavily sugared black coffee. "So start at the beginning, Aditi, and for God's sake, do you have to bounce so loudly," he grumbled. His brow furrowed as his head continued to throb, but he felt less likely to keel over.

"I'll be gentle," whispered Aditi, momentarily putting her finger to her lips to divide a deep red colored cupid's bow. "I got your details from Avni, told her that I was coming to visit and asked her to keep it quiet."

Devan tutted and shook his head. Only he winced with the motion. "Don't know what hurts more," he said, "the hangover, or my mother being complicit and in this."

"I packed a bag, boarded a plane," continued Aditi. "I drove through the night to come find you. Only the whole place seemed to be in a full-scale party," she looked out the window a moment and watched the crowd. Outside, the street was thronging with the fair kicking off. The people of Peace were out and about, amassed to soak up the carnival atmosphere. "So I dumped my stuff at the B&B and made some discreet inquiries," Aditi turned back to him and smirked. "It turns out that there aren't many Anglo-Indian gentlemen 'round these parts. The one in question was spotted partying up the road."

Devan set his coffee down, and tried to process the tidbits that Aditi was feeding him and slowly. "Still doesn't explain," He said with a sigh, "How I came to be completely blotto and yet managed to get home. Then there is the Stetson, the toffee apples. The pink boa!" exclaimed Devan and loudly.

"Hold on," Aditi slid her hand into the pocket of jacket and pulled out crumpled up pieces of paper. "Here," she said, smoothing out a few and sliding them across the table towards him. "There was a date auction."

"Date?" he was about to ask, but saw how much she had paid for him; how much he had cost.

"Given how hammered you got, Devan Coultrie," said Aditi, crossing her arm. "You really aren't a cheap date."

Tutting loudly, Devan winced once and with feeling. His head was in the throes of a full drum and bass session, or so it felt. "That is cheap, and a half the price," he tried to laugh but it pained him as he jabbed a finger at the receipt. "A few dollars more would not have hurt you, my head on the other hand," there was a deep groan as he rubbed his temples. "You'd think I was damaged and dented with being so cut price."

"You are a bit," squeaked Aditi, snorting with glee.

"Don't," said Devan, he had an inkling as to where this might lead. "I'm not a complete lemon," he added. "I'm happy, healthy and trying to find my bit of peace."

"Did it have to be here though," asked Aditi, looking at him intently and her lashes fluttering. She picked up the clutch of receipts and returned them to her pocket. "Peace, Montana and proper cowboy country. Maybe you have watched too many westerns. A-ha!" she was squealing again, and loudly. "Maybe that's how you won the Stetson!"

Throwing his hands into the air, Devan shrugged. "Boa?" he asked, putting his hand to his coffee.

Aditi bunched up her shoulders and also shrugged. "Can't remember that exactly," she shook her head and stuck out her bottom lip. "You were a bit, you know…"

Retreating to Peace

"…Hammered," nodded Devan. "We've established that." He noisily slurped his coffee and drained the cup. "Let's make a move, might be able to take in what's left of the fair. You can get the bill," he said rising from his seat and making towards the door. He left Aditi to settle the bill, and maybe offer Laura some intrigue.

He stood outside and waited for a few moments. Main Street really was busy. The Founder's Day weekend had drawn people out and about; this was the heartbeat of Peace.

"Apparently, there's a fortune teller," Aditi pronounced as she stepped out of the diner and linked her arm around his. "Come on, let's go find her; we can see what the future holds."

Devan found himself being dragged along, whilst being mesmerized by those that he passed by. He didn't need a fortune teller to divine the future, he already knew. His future was here and right in front of him. His fortune was in Peace and that was the way it was going to be.

Chapter 11

Usually, Devan was woken by birdsong. Great Aunt Claudie had painfully thin walls and the ceiling may as well have been made of eggshell. He didn't need to set an alarm as the dawn chorus was always bang on time. Except today; today he couldn't hear a single thing as he woke and turned on his side. There was serenity in the silence that shrouded him as he slowly opened his eyes. The silence reminded him that he wasn't in his own bed, but a bed that belonged to another. Technically, the bed belonged to the Peace B&B. He was not alone either; the other occupant was a deeply slumbering brunette named Aditi.

Retreating to Peace

As she slept, Aditi's face was completely blank. There was nothing to suggest a tumultuous nightmare or frenzied fantasy that might crease her brow. Devan noticed a black eyelash that was sat on the bridge of her nose, somewhat spoiling the enthralling image of a sleeping beauty. Moving his hand from beneath the covers, he dabbed a finger to his tongue and then pressed it against the lash to remove it. Moving his finger to his lips, he blew the lash away and made a wish.

This was what happened when you had history with someone. If you did not learn from it, you were doomed to repeat it.

Devan had a vague plan. He would do what he did the last time; he would walk the walk of shame. He would leave; quickly, quietly, without making as a sound. Aditi would be left sleeping alone as he made his return to Great Aunt Claudie. His previous attempt in doing this had been fairly successful, to repeat it couldn't be so difficult.

Pushing the light weight duvet away, he slowly sat up and swung out his long legs to land his feet to the floor. His boxers had somehow stayed where they were supposed to; Devan rolled his eyes skywards in silent thanks. For a moment, his heart had quickened. He would have remembered if things had gone in that particular direction again. Looking over his shoulder, Devan made sure that Aditi was still asleep. If she stayed asleep, she was less likely to haul him backwards and once more into the soft depths of her arms. Sliding off the firm mattress, he listened carefully. There was nothing as awkward as creaky springs to give you away and when you wanted to make a quick escape.

Threading on his jeans that had lain crumpled in a heap on the floor, Devan didn't fight the soft smile that was spreading across his face. He had no regret about the last time that he had ended up in Aditi's arms; there were certainly no regrets this time either. As he tugged on a pair of blue and white socks, Devan shrugged. There had been no fade to black this time. There might have been, had he not been so tired or fallen asleep so quickly. Such was the luxury of a proper bed-yes, he was going to blame the bed-a stark comparison to his own in the caravan. Had he not slipped out of Aditi's arms and into a sudden sleep, he might have been fishing his boxers out from below the bed. Searching below the bed, that was where Devan found his blue and green checked shirt. Picking up his shoes, he padded softly out of Guest bedroom 5. Closing the door quietly behind her, Devan narrowed his eyes as it met the frame. Then his pace quickened, and with his shirt unbuttoned and chest bared he ran down the stairs.

Other than not wanting to face Aditi, he had another reason to run and at a pace. In about forty minutes, Devan was scheduled to meet an architect. After months of anticipation, the farmhouse was now structurally sound and would be de-cloaked of the green plastic that had shrouded it. Today was the day that he would finally get to wander around inside and properly. Thoughts of last night's encounter with Aditi jostled around inside his head, competing with the plans that he had made for the farmhouse.

There was a third thought that was starting to form in his head. A thought underlined by a gut that made squelchy rumbling noises as Devan followed the curve of the staircase. Eventually he found himself at the bottom and on the ground floor. Standing in the foyer, he had the dining room to his right and the front desk directly ahead. Craning his neck towards the dining room, Devan's head and stomach collided. If he timed it right, Devan could nip in and then out having plundered something to eat. Technically, he wasn't exactly a paying guest, and this was taking something a liberty.

"I'm hungry," he muttered doing up his shirt as he held onto his Dr. Marten's beneath his arm. Devan casually walked into the dining room; he made a beeline for the bagels and cheeses and scooped some up into a serviette. As he moved, he saw something in his blind spot. "On the go," he said, waving his breakfast at the couple watching from their table.

Holding onto his plunder that little bit tighter, Devan scarpered back to the foyer and the front desk.

Dropping his shoes to the floor, he picked up a scrap of paper and a pen too. He scrawled an apology and a thank you; Devan also promised and in neat tightly formed handwriting that he would come by again and pay in full. Otherwise, the B&B might want to bill Aditi if they really wanted to. Signing his name and even adding Oakview below, Devan felt his soul feel a little less a flame. Jabbing his feet into his boots, he turned tail and quickly left the B&B. He had half an hour to get home and make himself look vaguely presentable.

Chapter 12

Aditi was one hell of a distraction that much was clear. As he arrived home, Devan was more than just a little out of breath. He didn't have long, but he could have a quick rinse down in the shower and before the architect arrived. The bagel that he had stolen from the B&B was thrown onto a worktop by the stove. It would be wolfed down when he tumbled out of the shower and was dripping all over the floor.

August was starting to kick off and the development of Oakview was moving apace. With the architect arriving, this meant the removal of the sea-green plastic that had cloaked the property. There had been a multitude of technical and significant re-modelling going on beneath the covers. Aditi had been here now two weeks having landed in the middle of the Founder's Day celebrations. For two weeks, the pair of them had loafed around Peace like two hormonally incandescent teenagers without a care in the world. Devan bit into the pilfered bagel whilst watching the window, and make short work of it. It was now that he could feel the nagging feeling of guilt. If this wasn't such an important meeting, he would have stayed beneath that duvet and with Aditi. They would have spent another day wandering from one side of Peace to the other; all with typical English wide-eyed awe at the quaintness of everything.

It had taken him two weeks to end up half dressed and submerged entirely in Aditi's arms. Devan arched his brows as he dispensed the now crumpled up serviette into a waste bin. He had been perfectly stone cold sober; they had both been, there were no excuses at all. They had spent the day in Billings, organizing on going bits and pieces for the renovations. Being with Aditi, with his best friend in this whole world had felt comfortable. Devan had actually let his guard down; for the first time in months, he had felt as though he was able to breathe. He had also been able to laugh, to see the future and the grey clouds that clung to his skin felt as though they had been lifted.

Retreating to Peace

Grey clouds that had been around ever since Carly had died and had felt stuck in place. And there it was; his heart plummeted from being really very high and landed somewhere next to his kidneys with something of a hefty squelch. Devan spotted a moving smudge on the far of the window, the architect had arrived in a black sedan that was now being parked just to the RV. As he left Great Aunt Claudie, Devan felt his 'phone pulsate in the pocket of his jeans. He knew exactly who it was; she would have to wait. For now, he was back to the whole retreating to Peace plan. Peace was his priority, and not a hormonally incandescent moment of madness.

The floor plan of Oakview Farmhouse had been unfurled and lay flat across the still warm bonnet of Cara Mason's black sedan. Devan moved his hands to anchor the top and bottom right hand corner. Just above the sheet and by the windshield wipers, there were two cups of coffee that had been freshly made. He and Cara had exchanged pleasantries. Given how much this was costing him, Devan was eager to get down to business.

Tracing an index finger around the wall of the dining room, Devan carefully studied the floor plan. "It's all well and good showing me in black and white, Cara, but I would rather just go on inside. Then I can have a proper look," said Devan, leaning forward and using his hand span to measure the distance between the lounge and the breakfast bar. "I really want to get the kitchen done," he said tapping the words that were centered between his lounge and the breakfast bar. "It arrives in two days. Help a boy out would you, Cara," he pleaded, just as he felt his pocket pulsate once again. Devan tutted loudly as he peered into his pocket. His damned 'phone was heating up and against the lining of his pocket as Aditi was calling him and non-stop.

"Girlfriend?" Cara asked and all too pointedly. "Guess she would like the kitchen sorted too."

"Friend," snapped Devan, looking directly at the freckle faced blonde that stood before him with a thunderous expression. "And she wouldn't know what to do with it. Aditi burns water and curdles milk. Show me my kitchen, Cara. A boy's gotta eat," he said, his tone and expression both softening. He put his hand to his pocket, Aditi was calling again. "And you know, properly too. That coffee I made you," Devan waggled both of his index fingers towards the two mugs sat on the bonnet. "It's probably a bit crappy and then some."

"I wasn't going to say, but it is…" Cara's eyes crinkled up at the corners as she laughed quietly and nodded. "All right, we could go on in," she said gathering up the floor plan and then waving it in the direction of the house ahead. "For the sake of future coffees, let's open her up. The covers are due to fly off today anyone."

Retreating to Peace

"Atta girl!" exclaimed Devan, reaching for his own mug and draining it onto the ground. "Lead on then. Tell me what I am making my Peace with. This has been a long time coming, I'm telling you."

Chapter 13

Having handed Devan the coiled up blue print, Cara used both hands to pull apart a curtain of blue-green plastic from across the front door. She did so with ease and her bright fuchsia pink nail polish escaped unharmed from the abrasive and heavy sheeting. "Hold onto your hat," Devan," Cara said grinning and adjusting the yellow one that sat on her coiled up and away hair.

Clutching the floor plan to his chest, Devan could feel his heart race and towards a crescendo. In his stomach, figurative butterflies fluttered and flew around and threatened to herniate something. He was about to step forwards, when his put his hand to his pocket. The plan had been to do this alone. "Cara, could you…could you, could just give me a minute. I, um, would like to make a call," he said, hearing himself stutter like a child over his words.

Nodding, Cara moved off ahead through the door that she had opened. "Sure, I'll be in the kitchen," she said disappearing off into the darkness. "Just follow the floor plan and get your bearings."

"Thanks," he said reaching into his pocket and taking a hold of his 'phone dialed Aditi's number. "Stop," he got straight in as the call was taken and a tirade of abuse started. "You can kick my backside from to here to Timbuktu, but save it for later..."

"Oh?" replied Aditi, pausing in her volley of abuse.

Devan gulped and stepped over the threshold. "Come to the house," he said, "I've just stepped in-"

"And you would like me to hold your hand, would you?" asked Aditi, her tone raised and burred abrasively. "You really have no shame do you, Devan?"

"Please," whispered Devan, feeling a full flurry of butterflies swirled around his spleen. "Lend me your hand, Aditi, just this once? I'm scared, and I could really do with some moral support."

Hearing the call disconnect, he let out a hot breath. The burring sound of dead air made it pretty clear as to how Aditi felt about holding his hand. Puffing out his chest, he drew in dusty air and tucked the 'phone back into his pocket. With Aditi's refusal, a blister had formed in his stomach. "Serves me right, I guess," he told himself. "Karma really is a cow," added Devan as he moved into the lounge and headed towards the kitchen. As he moved, he unfurled the floor plan to hold it out in front of him. Devan walk slowly, so that he might orientate himself and get some form of bearings as he moved. For now, the recently lain floor beneath his feet was pale grey concrete. He hoped to eventually fit the whole of the ground floor with dark, wooden, durable flooring. Devan positioned himself between the space labelled dining room and the kitchen. Cara was standing a little further up ahead where he imagined having a traditional range cooker. The one that he had ordered was white with shiny yellow handles and there was the huge great big, beefy, 'fridge that he had also found in Billings.

As he lowered the plan a little, he caught sight of Cara standing with her hands on her hips and looking sidelong at him.

"Will the boy eat?" she asked, "And properly?"

"I hope so," replied Devan, grinning a little, his cheeks bloomed with childlike glee. "It's a good size," he added, starting to walk around and with the plan raised aloft. "Much bigger than I am used to, and also what I expected to be honest. So much that could happen here," he pivoted a little to take in the breakfast area.

Retreating to Peace

"Family?" Cara queried, fiddling with her hard hand and venturing towards him. "Food, fun, maybe the odd fight?" she posed, laughing and loudly.

"Food definitely," agreed Devan. He laughed unreservedly. The sound of their throaty humor bounced across the naked walls. "Family maybe," he couldn't help but shrug, the thought was still too painful to think about. "There was a plan, but it sort of fell through."

Cara looked at him and sideways once again. "With the, er, friend, who called earlier?" she asked, sounding as if she was on a permanent fishing expedition.

"Friend?" asked Devon, confused and with his brow creased. "Who, Aditi, oh no," he shook his head and firmly. "No, not her, someone else; I made plans with Carly." He dipped the floor plan and rolled it up. "Carly, was my partner, and we were together long enough to plan families, and fun…only," he paused and let out a constrained breath. "She died, and the plans, they all sort of went poof!" he jabbed the plan into the air for emphasis and gave a deep shrug. "I had to change the plans, our plans, and come up with my own. So I thought about to coming to Peace-retreating to Peace-to well, find it. Get some peace." He had never said that out loud; hearing it, and bounce across the walls was slightly unnerving.

Standing shoulder to shoulder with him, Cara had move closer and closer as she listened. "I'm sorry," she said quietly. "It all sounds as though it was a really tough time."

"It was, yes," replied Devan, "Thank you. It's all been a bit trying, to be honest. An interesting process too, and getting here," he waggled the plan and crossed his arms. "Standing here, I'm trying to get my head around it all. Cara, would you mind," he ventured, raising the rolled-up plan. "If I flew solo, had some time alone and just got a better feel for the place."

"Of course, this is your home!" Cara almost sang the words, "Go ahead," she said stepping away. "Everything is ready to go for you. I'll go check in with the contractors." Cara headed towards the lounge, and spoke over her shoulder. "We can get all the sheeting down, and make it all look pretty for you. I'm on my cell if you need me. Plan away, have all those hopes," she said finally, waving as she disappeared around a wall.

"And dreams!" he called out after her. As Cara left, Devan was alone with his thoughts and took a few moments to take it all in. This was his, all his and his patch of Peace.

"All mine," Whispered Devan, "But what the flip do I do with it, and shouldn't I share it with someone, someone special?"

Chapter 14

With the floor plan coiled up and tucked under his arm, Devan trudged up a bare staircase. As he climbed up, he noted the roughness of each and every step. He remembered the images that the Realtors had sent him; the stairs had been wooden and there were a few panels missing. These had now been replaced with all of the flight stripped back to nakedness. "Carpet or varnish, that is the question," Devan mused as he arrived at the top.

The blank barrenness that filled downstairs was mirrored upstairs and on the landing. He was stood in the middle of a long and thin corridor with the master bedroom at one end and the third bedroom at the other.

Unfurling the floor plan, he once more had to orientate himself. Having turned it around a few times, he shuffled off towards the master suite. On paper, the room looked huge, cavernous almost. As he entered he noted a door leaning against the wall; he'd forgotten about some of the materials that survived and were being given a new lease of life. Heading towards the window, he looked out and saw Great Aunt Claudie and his shipping container. That would need to emptied, there would decorating and furnishing; a lot was needed to make this house a home.

"What is that you want exactly?"

The sharpness of Aditi's tone broke Devan's silent reflection. Such was the edge that he snapped his head quickly in the direction of her voice. She stood there before him in something of a Warrior Queen stance and a face dark with indignation. He was struck by two things as his mind failed to send word to his lips. Firstly, the power of her words; his feet felt as though they had been nail gunned to the floor. Secondly, her hair was pulled back in to a bedraggled pony tail to present her face in full light. She wasn't wearing a single solitary scrap of makeup, and the fury that her voice carried made her skin glow.

"Well," asked Aditi, audibly huffing as she strode across the floor towards him and snatched the floorplan from his hands. "Don't just stand there. You asked that I get here," she added, her tone becoming more abrasive and burred. She looked directly at him, her eyelashes fluttering and fanning. "Come here and hold your hand, when what I should do, is smack your backside from here to Timbuktu," Aditi puffed out her cheeks, and the floorplan trembled in her hands. "Trouble is, you might actually enjoy it," Aditi tutted sharply. "Leaving a lady's bed… and like that." Aditi curled up the paper and held it as though she was about swat him around the head. "You really are a crap-hole, Coultrie."

Still he watched, completely and utterly transfixed. Devan was mesmerized by the way that Aditi wore anger and disdain across her face. Her nostrils had flared, and her face was a mixture of flushed pink and olive. He scanned his eyes across the tightly held shoulders that rose and fell as she fumed quietly. All he could feel was power, pure heat that radiated towards him with the heat of a furnace. He had two options: to walk in or to walk away.

He was still trying to flip the figurative coin as Aditi slowly drew her eyes up and prepared to nail him to the floor once again.

"What?" she asked, brows raised as high as his hackles.

Taking a stride forward, Devan pried the floor plan from her fingers and threw it across the room. From the corner of his eye, he saw it flutter to the floor. The next thing that he knew, he was on auto pilot and pulling her close so that they were lip-locked. He could taste strawberry lip balm, smell the combination of jasmine fabric softener and sweetly spiced perfume that clung to Aditi's skin. Devan heard the thudding of his own heart and the shuffling of Aditi's feet as she curved into his chest. He curled a leg around hers, as he felt himself sway.

They were both about to lose their center of gravity; he really didn't want to fall, but he could feel the pull and it was getting stronger and stronger.

Aditi clearly had other ideas and kneed him directly; the aim to distort the strength of gravity and draw him closer into the depths of her arms.

Devan's center of mass finally caved in. The two of them fell- a mixture of legs and arms- hard with an almighty thud upon the cold, hard, dusty floorboards. With bodies at right angles to one another, they were conjoined in a human heap.

His lips were his own once more as they parted, and were pulled into a wince. Devan felt the weight of her stare, as she looked at him down her nose. He went almost cross eyed in trying to focus and uncurled fingers that had been pressed firmly into her hip to rub the back of his head. Still his heart was beating, racing as though supercharged; his blood however was surging and in an interesting direction. He drew his legs close and looked at the gap where the door might have been.

Aditi moved a hand towards face and tilted his jaw towards her. Her other hand and moved from his neck and was making a descent south.

"Seriously?" ventured Devan, feeling his one head and the other throb. "There is no door and for the sake of decency; not mention the splinters."

"I'm not the screamer," Aditi purred, a hint of laughter escaped her lips. Her hand was still travelling and about to break and enter his jeans. "Everyone is outside and otherwise engaged," she said having found his fly.

Devan's eyes narrowed, his wince had well and truly disappeared. There it was again, the power, the pull and the sheer passion that Aditi could flick on like a switch. Power that pulled him into her arms and rendered him helpless. What was the worst that she might do to him? She might want to kick his backside from here to Timbuktu and that was her prerogative all things considered. For how, he would suffer the splinters. This was his house, his home; he could do what he wanted. Half an hour and they might just make it to the kitchen.

Chapter 15

It was fortunate that the walls had been skimmed; it was less fortunate that they were a rather ugly shade of chestnut. Things would however change; Devan would make sure of that. Standing on the one but last rung of a ladder, he was painting the ceiling of the master bathroom and a fairly neutral shade of Magnolia. Most of the paint had made it to the surface above his head, but had also dripped into Devan's hair and stubble. Drops and starburst clung to his face and made him look rather like a badly made up clown. Passing a weighty roller across the ceiling, he wore a look of dogged determination. He was applying a second and final coat, the next phase was to tile the walls. Boxes of pale blue tiles sat in the corner where a shower would eventually be fitted. Behind Devan and below the window was a bath, resting in peace and covered by a thick, heavy, grey sheet. He looked over his shoulder at the heap and shook his head; there was still an awful lot of work to be done. Choosing the bathroom had been a somewhat interesting experience.

Aditi had laughed with both mischief and menace as she pushed him towards the display model. "You have to get a bath," she had said. "You can have a shower as well, no problem. Your roof, your money, your rules; but we all need a bath from time to time. Try it," she had poked her fingers into his shoulders and nudged him further still.

"I don't want to try it," he had protested. His words fell on deaf ears as his Dr. Marten's met with the panel beneath the bath. Devan found himself lurching forward, the reflex being to plant his hands onto the side of the bath.

It didn't take much as he was nudged forward and clambered into the tub. His slight but gangly six foot frame was neatly tucked into the bath, with his legs crossed over the plug hole. Placing his hands on the sides, he looked up at Aditi who stood beside the tub. "I don't want to get one," Devan rolled his shoulders with a deep shrug.

Aditi really was looming over him, and her eyes were glimmering with mischief. The mischief had been there ever since she had dragged him out to go shopping. She had coaxed and cajoled him out of his bed in the RV and demanded that they go out to buy fixtures and fittings. All he was to bring with him was his wallet; his job was just to agree with everything; he was not to argue. She momentarily stuck out her tongue and pulled a face before letting her gaze travel down his legs and towards his feet.

"Oi!" he exclaimed, pulling his feet back and drawing his knees to his chest. "If I stood there and mentally undressing you, you would have my bits for breakfast. Stop," he added, raising a hand and waggling an index finger. "And no," said Devan, keeping his knees close to his chest. "It doesn't have to be big enough for two. I don't share my shower. I'll be damned if I have to share my bath, Aditi."

"Spoilsport," she whispered, leaning forwards with her hands clamped to the side of the bath. "Don't bloody move," she uttered, swooping in and plundering a kiss in pure spontaneity.

Caught off guard, Devan had pulled his hands from his legs and flailed them around. Before long, he had given in and cradled her face. There was no point in resisting. "You're not road testing this thing with me, and in public," he said having been allowed to catch his breath. As Aditi moved away, he cambered side to side in the bath; it wasn't exactly comfortable. "Help me out, would you?" he asked, holding out his hand so that he could be hauled out.

"But you said no!" Aditi squealed, stepping further away from the bath and with her hands raised in defiance. "What's a girl to do, when you said that you wouldn't share and in public. Much rather I helped you out and in private, would you?" she was laughing now, and wildly. So much so that other customers were looking at them and quizzically at that.

As Aditi backed away, Devan was making something of a dog's dinner in trying to clamber out of the bath head first. "You wait 'til I get to the tiles." He said loudly and dramatically to a now captive audience. "They won't be the only thing to be laid and properly," he had trilled the last bit. Having got to his feet, Devan curled an arm around Aditi and pulled her towards him rather unapologetically.

Lowering the roller from the ceiling, Devan felt his face burn and passed his palm over his jaw. As he stepped down from the ladder, he took another look at the stack of tiles. Hugging the roller close, Devan arched his brows as the process of choosing tiles drifted into his mind.

"I don't get it and once again," he had said whilst he stood in aisle. Devan held a tile squarely in his hands.

"How is that shade of white, better than this shade of white?" he was genuinely perplexed as Aditi decided to stand behind him and encircle him with his arms. "I would rather they were blue, to be honest," he added, as he felt the warmth of her body against his. He could also smell the heady and intriguingly intoxicating scent of Aditi's spiced scent. A scent that over the last few weeks had wafted around the RV; it had settled on his skin and was quite firmly wedged inside his head.

"Do you promise?" Aditi whispered and into his ear. Her teeth were almost settled upon his ear lobe and she rose on her tip toes to get closer still. "To lay the tiles, me, and properly?" she continued, pressing her teeth into the fleshy skin of his ear. He could feel her hot breath caress the back of his neck. "Say you do. That you want to."

Aditi's hands had started to travel and from his waist. He remembered watching her tapered fingers move to the tops of his jeans. The smell of her perfume was becoming increasingly more intense, fueling the beating of his heart. Not only was chest feeling tighter, there was a movement and a quickening of a sort below stairs.

He had dropped the tiles onto a nearby shelf. A glassy clink had signaled their escape and back to the car. Luckily, they had already paid for the bath.

Tapping the roller handle. Devan let out a very deep, very long breath. Stepping across the bathroom, he pressed a palm against the window sill to have a quick look outside and get some fresh air; the window was open for ventilation. He tried to look over his shoulder, and felt a sharp pull as he moved. Lifting the collar of his t-shirt, he peered beneath the fabric. He saw that there was a bruise, and it was going from blue to green, having initially been sunshine yellow. He had been laid, and properly at that.

Other than wanting air, he had headed to the window to see take a good look at the view. Another moment of afternoon delight was associated with the clutch of oaks that could be seen from the window. The bathroom floor had given him bruises across the breadth of his shoulders. An oak beside the walled garden had given him bark burn and blisters on a different part of his anatomy entirely. Propping the roller up against the cloaked bath, Devan felt dry scratchiness in his throat. He had been at this for ages, his stomach was growling in concert with thirst that made him smack his lips together. Hunger, thirst and a throbbing memory of what happened at the base of the oak would distract a man.

Leaving the bathroom, Devan's paint splattered work boots traipsed across the landing, down the stairs and thudded across flooring that had only been laid a few days ago. He headed to the newly installed kitchen and pulled open the door of a fridge that was distinctly taller and wider than he was. Grasping at a can of lemonade with one hand, he slid out a plate of sandwiches with the other. Elbowing the 'fridge closed, Devan headed out the door that led the walled garden that jutted out the kitchen. For now, the walled garden was filled with empty terracotta pots and didn't particularly float his boat.

He wanted to eat his lunch beneath an oak, a very specific oak. Beneath his feet, wooden steps gave way to what were easily seventy different shades of green and beautifully lush blades of grass. He had looked out here whilst having breakfast and there had been dew covering it all. Each and every blade of grass had shimmered and shone as though a precious jewel as he walked in the direction of the oak that was nestled beside the walled garden. The distance between the wall and the tree had made the episode of afternoon delight a truly private but passionate escapade. The bark burn was one thing, but no one ever mentioned grass stains or grass burn for that matter when going a little in *flagrante delicto*.

Devan trudged towards the oak. The tree had been there so long that its roots had raised a ridged mound at its base. Letting out a slow, dry and thirsty breath, he sat himself down beneath the boughs and stretched out his legs through blades of grass. Resting the plate of sandwiches on his flat for now stomach, he tugged at the ring pull of the canned lemonade nestled next to his hip.

Retreating to Peace

A breathy hiss escaped the can, and echoed in his imagination those that had accompanied getting splinters and grass stains. Sliding the cellophane from the sandwiches, he felt his mind wander as he relived the episode below the tree.

"This is not some Mills and Boon's book," he had said, whilst being pulled at speed down wooden steps and out of the walled garden. Compliant and not yet complaining, he followed Aditi as they hurtled around the wall of the house.

"Harlequin and over here," Aditi responded, letting go of his hand as they arrived by an oak and firmly landing her hands onto his shoulder blades. "And no one will see, this is private property; your private property." Then she pushed him forward with force.

Stretching out one hand as he flew forward, he turned and pulled Aditi down with the other. Devan felt the ground beneath him and tried to forget what it might be crawling with.

"The barn next," cackled Aditi as she tumbled into his arms and onto the rest of him. There were worst things that he might be sandwiched between. "You actually have one, just like the sodding books," she added, turning to face him and flatten out his hands to pin him down. "So you know, for now…."

"Lie back and think of England?" asked Devan, arching his brow as quick work was made of his fly being unbuttoned.

Bringing the lemonade to his lips, Devan took a mouthful of the sweet, tangy, fizzy liquid and savored the sugariness. No doubt it would rot his teeth and the rest of his insides. The flaring of the sun mean that was too hot for tea, too early for a beer; there was nothing as harmless as a cold can of lemonade. There was dinner later; Aditi had persuaded him to accompany her to an estate well beyond Billings. She needed a wingman whilst she schmoozed a gathering of sharks in suits. He had zoned out when she had started to talk about litigation, pro-bono property managed and how this was a condition attached to her on going sabbatical out here in Montana. As attractive as her brain was, the legalese that Aditi spouted rather made his head spin.

Devan sat for a while, slowly nibbling at the perfectly chilled ham and cheese sandwiches. He would have to graze on something later. Aditi had mentioned something about a wine reception. There was no part of him that wanted to dangle from her arm whilst deliriously drunk and bordering on debauched.

The later on came sooner than he had expected. He couldn't help it. He had rather enjoyed the wine reception, enjoyed it little too much in fact. Devan was drunk and most definitely so. Inebriation rather made dancing a bit more difficult as Aditi's arms curved around and clamped his body in place next to hers. Devan did his best not to be knocked sideways across a parquet floor beneath low level lighting as a band let their bass kick in.

"You didn't have to drink so much and so fast," Aditi hissed and through pearly white teeth. "You know what bubbles do to you. Did you even eat anything today?" she asked, kicking his ankle with a strappy stiletto so that he might sway and not stagger to betray his level of intoxication.

"I did, hic," nodded Devan, putting two fingers to his lips and looking rather sheepish. "Sorry," he whispered. "I'll behave," he added, unable to suppress a rather raspberry infused burp.

"You'd better," tutted Aditi as she swatted his shoulder with the back of her silver, beaded clutch. "You just wait, Devan Coultrie, and until I get you home."

Chapter 16

Yellow ones, green ones, scalloped ones; there were even a couple that looked a lot like flying saucers. Devan put down a basket of patty pan zucchini onto his kitchen table and took a step back to look at the harvest. The middle of August was a bountiful time as the vegetable plot near the entrance of Oakview yielded an assortment of crops. He had been pleasantly surprised really, but the harvest that occupied entirely the dining table that sat eight was all too much for him alone. There was only so much ratatouille one boy could eat, this would all need a good home or several at least for it all to be eaten.

Retreating to Peace

"Flaming aubergines. If you don't like them, why grow them?" said an almost shrill voice behind him, his thought process was entirely derailed.

Devan turned to face the door that led to the wall garden and saw Aditi walk in. Cradled in her arms and looking very much like newborn babies, were a clutch of aubergines. Some were purple, long and elongated. Others were white and rounded. He really did despise them; in his mind, an aubergine was a vile creature and the almighty's idea of a joke.

"Fancied having a go," said Devan, moving towards her and liberating some of the aubergines before they landed onto the floor. "Live and learn, Aditi, otherwise things get a bit boring." With three aubergines in his hands, he went back to the table and added them to the bounty. "So much stuff," he said, his eyes stretching out wide as he ran a hand through his hair and across his scalp. As he let out a breath, he felt his chest being engulfed by Aditi's arms and the scent of strawberries wafted to his nose. Almost by reflex, he put his hand to hers and let it rest with her fingers intertwined with his.

For a moment, he was lost. But there was something nagging at him, and he slowly moved her hands from his breastbone to then shuffle from her reach. "We need to talk, Aditi," he said gently, pulling out a chair and sitting. He pulled out a second and nodded for her to take the hint.

Aditi's normally quite placid and doe-eyed expression changed immediately. Her lips appeared to thin out, narrow and the pout positioned to kiss him petered out entirely. She landed the aubergines that she had been left with heavily onto the table and took the proffered seat next to Devan. Crossing her legs, Aditi clasped her hands around her knees and wore a steely eyed game face. There was an intensity brimming in her eyes; the carefree glimmer that made them sparkle had fluttered away in an instant.

Once again, Devan found himself completely and utterly transfixed as he watched her move, sit and now eyeball him. Up to now, he had hung on her every word. Devan had absorbed every whisper, every breath and giggle. He had let things go as they had floated around Peace and fixed up the house. As he sat with her and with the silence hanging between them, Devan could feel words flutter and form in his mind. A battle Royale was occurring between his heart, his head and his gut so that he might have the courage to say what he felt. He watched Aditi's lashes bat and flutter, and raised his eyebrows as he watched her head tilt to the side in anticipation. He dropped his gaze and to the hands that she had wrapped around her knees, Devan remembered how her hands had pressed against his shoulders at a quarter to eight this morning.

Retreating to Peace

An hour later, the 'phone had rung and how Devan wished now that he had not taken that call.

"Chris called," started Devan, his words tumbling out and tremoring. "He wants to know what to do with your stuff as according to him, we are quote shacking up together unquote. Oh, and apparently, as I'm the son of a bachelor that you've been mooning over for years, I am welcome to you. I'm damaged, you're damaged, and crap happens." He drew in breath; breath caused his lungs to fall down inside his chest. "You've not been taking his calls, your mum gave him an earful and your cat misses you. He's thinking of putting her to sleep, do you want her?" As he stopped, he wiped the back of his left hand across his mouth. His lips and throat were now painfully dry; his heart was beating so hard that his chest felt as though it might burst. There were no more words for the moment the air seemed to crackle enough with anything else being poured into it. If he was to say more, the words would have been thorn-like with serrated edges and difficult to pass through his lips.

Aditi's eyes had become wider still at the mention of her on-off boyfriend. Her lips twitched to speak as she sat back and released her knee from her grip. Her hands fell to her sides rather despondently. She frowned, and opened her mouth to speak. "Devan-"

"Stop," said Devan made no apology for interrupting. "This has got to stop. This, this is not how it is supposed to be," he continued, lowering his head and shaking it. "What you and I are doing, what we have been doing over the last few months, Aditi, not one bit of it makes sense," he drew in breath and threw his hands into the air. "Can you tell me, since when were we together? Since when, was it me and you. I came here and to get over Carly-"

"I'm definitely not Carly," this time it was Aditi's turn to interrupt. "I will never be Carly; I will never be that woman. You are lying to yourself. Do not tell me that you mean nothing, have felt nothing and that this is just a jump between the sheets."

As he listened, her words felt as though they were covered in equal parts salt and venom.

Aditi's nostrils flared and she continued, her gaze fixing him in place still. "If I'm running, then you have been the butterfly net that caught me," she said licking her lip and gulping. "As broken as you are, I don't remember you resisting as I tried to fix you. Not this morning, or last week and definitely not over the last month. This whole retreating to peace nonsense-yes, you talk in your sleep-get over it, Devan. Stop punishing yourself, stop feeling sorry for yourself. No amount of clinging to rainbows, butterflies and jam making in Montana is going to bring her back. Get out of this dark, brooding, woe is me fantasy and start living again. I refuse to be cast into a dead woman's shoes; saying the wrong woman's name in the middle of pure ecstasy, Devan. I cannot even begin to tell you how much that bloody well hurts."

Slowly, Devan drew his head up and met her gaze once more. She had noticed; once he had kicked himself, twice had no idea what he might have said. The third time had been incredibly stupid and was as recent as the unmade bed upstairs. In his head, in his world, Aditi and Carly had not just collided but morphed into one. He could no longer see the line that distinguished the two women. Boundaries had become blurred to the point where reality was starting to fracture.

"You're right," uttered Devan, his voice only just above a whisper. "You are most definitely not Carly. Carly, I loved to her bones. You, Aditi, not so much," he added shaking his head. "What with the feigned doe-eyed innocence and your propensity to dramatize everything without facing what makes you unhappy. I can admit to being broken, admit to a Band-Aid bunk up. Let's face it, that's what we've been doing and probably should snap out of it. I'm happy to stand still, and to fix my broken bits," he said, letting out a hot breath that felt bottled up inside. "You might want to stop running, as eventually the road ends. It ends, and you will find yourself freefalling from a cliff. That is going to hurt," he could feel his tone and hackles rise as he spoke. "And I'll be damned if I will become your bloody parachute. Stop bloody running, and get out of here."

He dropped his hands to the table before him and pushed himself to his feet. Feeling his heart race, there was also a dry, grainy coarseness in his throat. "This is over, Aditi," he gulped and passed the tip of his tongue across his lips. "You can scoff," continued Devan. "You can sneer and be as derogatory as you flaming well want to be. I want the rainbows, butterflies and jam making in Montana. All right," he shoved his chair forward and stood behind it.

"I don't get to do that with Carly, but I am not going to be so stupid, so short sighted as to do with it you. Go," he moved his hands from the chair and waved them at the door out. "I'm going to take a walk to the brewer's barn. I will be there for the rest of the day. I might pop back later for lunch. Just go, as I really don't want you to be here when I do. Go back to the B&B, another motel, I don't care, but go. You and me, Aditi, it's done, it's dusted. This daydream is over. What we have been doing all this time, it is over."

Pushing the chair closer still to the table, Devan used the exit out the walled garden himself. From his pocket, he removed a pair of dark sunglasses and put them on and strode off towards the brewer's barn sat directly behind the house. His priority had been the house, so all of the outbuildings on Oakview were all in need of repairing. As his chest felt tighter with sheer frustration, his mind whirred with potential plans. The brewer's barn he would keep for himself, but there were other buildings that could potentially be turned over for community use. He had plans for Oakview; plans that didn't involve Aditi or anyone else for that matter.

As he walked, Devan thought about jam making in Montana. He wanted the jam jars, the fabric covers and these danced around his brain at the speed of light. Retreating to Peace was his business and no one else's. Lost in his own world, Devan walked up to the door. As he tried to move it, it was heavy and not budging as quick as he would like. Grasping as the handle, he turned to shoulder barge it open and away from the frame. Devan was in a mood, and the buckling, blistered, bent up door took the brunt of it. The door surrendered to the onslaught of a black, thunder and lightning brimmed mood and creaked open. Cursing under his breath and rubbing his shoulder, Devan entered the building.

For the most part the barn was open plan as he looked up, he saw a mezzanine over-head. Light streamed in and at different angles; there were roof tiles missing above and the odd brick in the walls was absent too. There were oily rags here and there, bits of rusted down machinery and even the odd dead bird littered the floor. All that Devan could see was potential, never mind the detritus. There was so much that he might do with this barn; he could turn it into an office, a library or even a man-cave. All he had to do was think about it. His interest was however, piqued by the mezzanine. On the far side were steps leading up to it, and Devan picked his way across the uneven barn floor to head up. He negotiated the steps carefully, having to stretch his legs across a few gaps as he ascended the flight.

As he reached the top, he might have only taken a step or two as he tried to scan the mezzanine. Devan had stamped a foot, just to see how solid the floor was. He only wanted to check.

The last thing that Devan would remember was a creaking floorboard, his foot falling away from him and all six foot of him curiously object to gravity. He landed and with an almighty crash squarely in the center of the brewer's barn floor.

He was unconscious and for a while. Whoever found Devan would find him in a puddle.

Chapter 17

"Mr. Coultrie, you should probably wake," with a song like lilt, the voice was really quite soothing. The voice had a hand and it was sat gently on his shoulder trying to rouse him. "Your wife called, she's been calling on the hour, every hour. I did tell her to call back after you have had some lunch."

"Wife," murmured Devan, his one eye had opened and was just about focusing on a coffee and cream complexion that was framed by strands of honey blonde hair. It took a moment for Devan to register that he was being woken by a nurse, and then there was the whole wife thing. Opening his other eye, Devan tried to turn in the bed but felt a roaring sensation across his chest. That was probably the battered and broken ribs, he remembered something about that. Then there was the broken leg that bulged out from the bedsheets.

"But I don't have a wife," Devan said turning his face towards the nurse who had woken him. He squinted at her badge, to see her name. "I'm not married, Melody. Nice to see again, more painkillers please," he said with a yawn. She had woken him four hours ago to administer the pain relief, and now she was back. "And enough, with the Mister Cool-tree. The only Mister Cool-tree I know, is older, wrinkly and," he freed a hand from beneath the pale blue blanket that he lay under and waved it towards a white and green wall to his left. "Several thousand miles that way. Missis Cool-tree, is my mother."

"Ah!" Melody exclaimed, her rose bud lips shifted into something of a cat-like grin. "That explains the confusion with the switchboard," she said laughing quietly. "Your mother called too. Your wife-or not-was the one called Ad-it-ee. Av-knee Cool-tree, is your mum?" asked Melody, moving a wheeled tray table across his bed and close to his elbows.

He was being woken so that he could eat, be awake and take the next 'phone call. Sitting on the table was a white plastic dinner plate loaded with a pie and chips. This was after all a hospital, St. Vincent's in fact and this was where he had been brought with a broken, bloodied, bruised body.

Devan nodded slowly. "Avni," he said doing his best to sit up straighter. "There would be bells and whistles for her, if Aditi was my wife. God, I feel rough," he half growled as he felt his chest burn and eyed his lunch with some disdain. He wasn't sure if he wanted to eat the food in front of him.

It had been just under two weeks since Devan had landed onto the floor of the Brewer's barn. In that time, August had slipped away in a post bloom sulk and September had sauntered in. Devan had registered the change in seasons between snatches of pain and sleep, he was glad of having had a room with a view. The ride to the emergency room had been a terrifying, and disorientating; sounds, smells and shrieking voices had changed his reality at the time a swirling sea of sensory overload.

"You don't look it," Melody replied and with a wink. She tapped a jug of water that sat on the tray table, it happened to catch Devan's reflection.

Nerserbadyerself," Devan's words were rather strangled as he yawned and was able to get a hand to his mouth in time to be polite. He had been out cold for two days after the surgery on his leg. There had been fears about swelling on his brain as well as the blood loss that came from his femoral artery being sliced. These fears were allayed when he had woken up in something of a roaring fury. Devan had snapped his eyes open at some time around tea time and tried his damnedest to rip out all of the tubing and wires that he found himself encumbered with. He had turned the air electric blue in not being able to move his leg and leap out of bed.

A whole gang of nurses had appeared and out of nowhere, looking very much like the proverbial cavalry. Disorientated and dazed, he had felt a man very much under attack. Since then, he had some-what regained his composure and wasn't feeling so defensive. Smiling as Melody left, Devan now rather enjoyed being fussed over and by ladies in scrubs. He waved as she departed and then saw another woman fill the frame.

It was the hair that started the process. Salt and pepper locks that curled towards a soft jawline, interrupted by two coral discs sat at the figure's ear lobes. She had worn the brightest, fussiest of earrings for as long as he could remember. Avni Coultrie had enough Christmas themed ear rings for the whole of Advent.

"Mum!" exclaimed Devan, sitting up straighter still and groaning as he moved. "What in the name of God are you doing here?"

Avni Coultrie had moved with such speed and toward her son; her eyes had darted the full length of his bed to take in the extent of his injuries. It barely took any time at all for her to arrive at his pillow. "My child took a nosedive off of something stupid," she replied softly, pretending to cuff the back of Devan's head. "What I'm doing here, I'm here to look after you. You scared the bloody life out of me, out of your dad," Avni was speaking so quickly, her words merged together as she didn't take a breath between them and started to sob. "And then there's Aditi. Devan, you really are an idiot, do you know that? Poor girl, she kept us updated on the 'phone, but we just had to get here."

Devan's face had crumpled and contorted. A little boy lost, a little boy held out his hands and for a mother's embrace. "I do," he said through gulps and sobs, "Mum, it hurts; all of it and so much."

"Falling from a hay loft will do that to you, kiddo," said his father, arriving and standing opposite Avni. "First, you flaming well leave the country," tutted Richard, placing a hand delicately to Devan's shoulder. "Then, then you go and break bits of yourself. You were a bit broken to begin with anyway."

"That's what made him a cheap date."

Devan sobbed and sniffed, but managed to untangle himself from his mother's arms to see Aditi. She was there, and standing at the door holding an electric blue duffel bag. A blue duffel that had been stowed away in his shipping container. It was battered, scuffed, scratched and once upon a time had been used to carry his football kit. He wouldn't be playing football and any time soon.

Bleary eyed and aching all over, Devan had no idea how to look Aditi in the eye and without his heart hurtling towards the floor. He didn't need to think about it and too much. Before he knew it, he had blacked out and collapsed backwards into pillows.

Aditi had sent his blood flowing in the wrong direction yet again. Only this time, it wasn't consensual.

Post op complications, an infection and a strong one. Those were the words that Devan had heard when he had spoken with the doctor. He wasn't out cold for two days this time. In a matter of hours, Devan was cautiously revived and a bit woozy having been attached to a drip of IV antibiotics. The drugs were strong enough to make a small rhino think happy thoughts and see double. He wasn't a small rhino, and he wasn't seeing double. What he saw was Aditi and sat at his bedside clutching a scrunched-up ball of bogey filled tissue.

"I feel all very floaty," he said trying to focus and on her tear-filled eyes. Tentatively his slid across the bed and went to touch Aditi's arm. Only in his state of drug induced doziness, Devan missed entirely. "I see you, Aditi," Devan whispered somewhat hoarsely. "You are here, but I can't touch you. I-I'm sorry, Aditi, I didn't mean…" he blinked a few times, his own eyes were starting to well up; it was just too hard to focus.

Pressing his lips together, he drew in air to steady himself. "When I see you, and you are here. I will say sorry properly, I really will. You don't deserve to be crapped upon, you really don't. I refuse; refuse to do that to you. And Chris," he snorted away blobs of bogey. "Chris is a crap hole, a complete and utter horse's behind that you need to drop. He's not one and I'm not the one; please don't make me the one, Aditi. You deserve someone who will run with you, and not away from you, I ran and all the way to Peace, remember."

Aditi had listened, dabbed her eyes with her crumpled up tissue. She said nothing, and watched him intently.

"I'm stoned, aren't I?" he asked, gulping a mixture of snot and air.

Aditi nodded and bit her lip. "Just a bit," she replied.

"Okay," he said sighing. "Let me sleep it off," he continued. Devan slid out his hand once more and missed a second time as he tried to reach her. "Let me come to my senses. Take my parents with you, to the B&B. Get them to bill me and with bells on."

He drew back his hand and closed his eyes. Devan pretended not to see her or hear Aditi howl with heartbreak as she left. As stoned as he was, he knew that there were no excuses for being stupid, selfish and a downright shyster.

Chapter 18

The antibiotics and painkillers certainly made it easier to sleep; Devan didn't have the energy or inclination to fight his body or his mind. So he slept and he dreamt. Not of Aditi, as his heart might have wanted; he dreamt of Carly and what might have been. It was only as he slept that his two worlds crashed together so that he might pull them apart; pull the two worlds apart and fully understand what it was that he had to do.

Disco lights and a shimmering ball had him being pulled to the middle of a crowded and jostling dance floor. He had protested loudly, but Carly was having none of it.

Retreating to Peace

"You really think that I will see in the New Year and whilst sat down with a warm glass of wine," Carly had said before drawing him closer into her arms. She was his plus one-there had never been a doubt that she wouldn't be-at the firm's annual New Year's shindig. This was probably the fourth one that she had been to, so Carly knew the drill. Wearing a floor length beaded dress; she quite literally radiated beauty in the beams bouncing off the glitter ball whilst tripping the light fantastic.

Devan was drawn closer and closer, he felt his bow tie being tugged undone and be smoothed down against his lapels. Carly's arms were wrapped firmly around his waist and her perfume sedated his senses as they swayed to the music.

"I am but a figment of your imagination," Carly said softly and below the sound of a thumping bass. "You cannot hold me; you have kept me too long. Let me go." Her tone had become brittle and before long, her words had drifted away.

Devan had felt and seen her pull away into the swathes of white plumes made by dry ice. He could no longer feel the warmth of her body against his or smell the rose infused perfume Carly always wore. Feeling as though his heart had been torn from his chest, he pressed a hand to his breast bone. Looking down and at his hand, he saw his fingers covered and with the deep scarlet hues that only a broken heart and blood could produce. There was a big hole where his heart had been.

"We had to stop, Mr. Coultrie," he heard as a clear as a bell. "After forty minutes, there was nothing more that we could do. Carly had lost too much blood." Those were the words that would forever be branded into his memory and were gouged across his very being.

There was nothing more they could do.

As the image of Carly fluttered and faded away, Devan felt as though his arms were heavy and empty. He had nobody to hold onto; there was nobody. There was nothing to keep him safe, love him or fill his universe. Fixed, rooted to the floor, Devan couldn't move forwards so that he might search for Carly in the swirls of white smoke that surrounded him. The music had stopped; all of the revelers around him had floated away. All around him, there was nothing but a thick blanket of darkness. Standing there, he was alone with the fun and frivolity of New Year's nothing more than a whisper in the wind. A wind that was picking up, wildly at that to become a hanging gale that churned around him. Devan felt coldness descend upon him, chill him to the core and his heart beat slowed as though it wanted to give up the ghost.

"I've got you. I have always got you."

Feeling the touch of two hands being pressed against his stomach, Devan looked down to see tapered fingers.

Retreating to Peace

At the ends of which were nails painted bright fuchsia pink. The beat of his heart had started to quicken, and he could feel warmth radiate across his shoulders with the firmness of flesh behind it. Curves and contours felt solid behind him; but not those belonging to Carly. He knew every inch of Carly and backwards. These were different curves and not altogether unfamiliar. Devan knew these curves almost as well as Carly's.

"Let her go, she did say."

Devan followed the movement of the hands up and towards his bloodied chest. There, the fingers were deftly closing up the deep, angry gash that Carly's death had caused.

"I can't," Devan uttered and with his voice breaking. "She was my whole world. We were going to do this together. Build a whole new world, me and her."

"Let her go," said the Aditi-like apparition, her hands landing softly on his thudding and healed chest. "And build your world with me, better the devil that you know. Let yourself love, heal and be happy."

His eyes snapped open; Devan woke in something of a cold sweat. Lying there in his hospital bed, he felt as though he had been picked up from the mattress and flung back down from a great height. Every inch of him hurt, ached and throbbed. Not least because of the bruises, but because of Aditi. He was a prized pillock and there was only one thing for it. There was only one woman; that woman was Aditi. There was no one else, but Aditi.

Chapter 19

Aditi didn't return for three days. It took Devan that long before he called her and asked that she drive him home from St. Vincent's. Sat on the edge of his bed, Devan watched the door. He leg was bound up in a black and blue splint. Next to him were a pair of crutches. He had been asked if he wanted a wheel chair, but with a combination of male pride and bravado Devan had refused the offer. Plus, he didn't particularly fancy the idea of his parents or Aditi pushing him around. His mum and dad might have done that very well and over thirty-four years ago, but now they were out of practice. As for Aditi, he couldn't count on her not to throw him under a passing bus. Devan's efforts to get to his feet had also led him to falling out with the nurses; using his crutches involved practicing, as much as he could in the corridor. The staff seemed hell bent on either shepherding him back to his room or then supervising his every move as he shuffled down the corridor.

In defiance of Doctor's orders, Devan was discharging himself. He had seen to his hospital bill and had several heated discussions with his insurance provider. So much so, that after one conversation he had flung his 'phone at the door and nearly taken out a passing nurse. As angry as he was, Devan paid his bill and got on with things. He had come to Peace with a healthy bank balance, and he wanted to keep it that way. Financially and physically, the plan was to stay in one piece for as long as possible.

He had called Aditi this morning and after a short consultation with his doctor. Half way out of bed, Devan had pulled out his 'phone from the bedside cabinet and dialed her number. Aditi had decided to stay in his RV, with his parents being sent to the B&B. They would be flying back to Britain in a few days. They had been persuaded that he would okay, and that as a grown man he didn't need babysitters.

"Aditi," he had said, the call connecting. Devan had not known immediately what he might say. He had thought only of saying her name. For two minutes exactly, a heavy, stony, over-bearing, silence hung between them and on the line. This was just long enough for Devan to formulate his question.

"Could you pick me up please," he had asked, his tone sounding much like a child who had been sharply chastised. "I'm discharging myself, and I'd like to get home."

"What time?" Aditi queried, her question dangled on the line; she had sounded as though she was mentally checking for space in her diary.

"One-ish, according to the doctor," replied Devan. "All of the take home stuff should be done, final checks and things."

A click in the connection told him that Aditi had hung up, the line went dead. Taking a look at his 'phone, he put it back into the cabinet. It had felt strange, asking for but not receiving an answer. Devan wasn't panicked that she might not come, or feel excitement at the prospect of her turning up. He felt nothing, and that worried him just a little bit.

Chapter 20

At least she had taken his call and not rejected it.

Devan checked his watch every ten minutes; that was the only that dragged his eyes away from the door. He had just looked at it and noted that it was one forty-five exactly; that was the time at which Aditi walked into his room. She was dressed in a pair of dark blue skinny jeans, boots that were laced up to just below her knees and his navy-blue donkey jacket that rather matched her get up. Her shoulders were splattered with raindrops, reminding him of just how long he had been trapped in the hospital. Things had changed and not just with the weather. In Aditi's hands were a set of keys, he looked directly at the chunky fob. He realized why it looked familiar, she had driven here and in his car; that rather made his stomach flip.

Incapacitated as he was, Devan couldn't therefore argue with her about gear changes or her inability to accelerate. He knew that back home, Aditi drove a rather battered, toy like black Ford Fiesta sprint that always struggled to make it past fifty and in one piece. He had survived the barn; all he had to do next was to survive Aditi's driving. This would be an interesting ninety minutes. He said nothing as she handed him his crutches and then tugged at his elbow so that he might stand.

"It's really good to see you," he shoved his heart into his mouth to speak, and lurched to his feet. Devan put his hand to hers, and felt that her hands were cold, trembling too as he squeezed her fingers.

Aditi tutted, and flexed her fingers to throw away his. "Start shuffling," she told him. "I'll go check you out with the nurses. Apparently, you've been doing their heads in and they are glad to be shot of you."

As he gingerly took a few steps forwards, Devan looked at her with his brows knitted. With his face black and thunderous, he calculated the risk and decided not to check for sarcasm.

Saying goodbye and thank you to the nurses was somewhat bittersweet. Devan wore the best smile that he could muster as Aditi stood there impatiently with her arms crossed. Her sullenness continued as they slowly traipsed to the lift and got to into his car. He felt like a chastised child, and awkwardly uncomfortably as they had been escorted to the lot by a nurse. There was no part of Devan that relished a silent journey back to Peace, but he wasn't sure how he would puncture the black and foreboding atmosphere that swirled around them.

For a good twenty minutes, Devan kept his eyes front and center. It was that or watch the landscape whizz past as Aditi's foot refused to edge beyond seventy five miles an hour and on I-90. Had his one foot not been so duffed up, Devan would have taken his Toyota up to the full eighty that most people did on this route. As pretty as patches of dead sage bush were, he had also glanced at the speedo a few times and willed the car to crank up a little.

Then there were bursts of Country and Western that would intermittently crackle out from the radio. Devan wasn't averse to it per se; he had just hadn't been here long enough to know what was good, bad and vaguely palatable. He would take talk radio, thunderous rock and double-bass infused R 'n' B any day of the week and over the sound of harmonicas.

"I would go faster," said Aditi having caught his glance at the wheel. "But I might put you through the windscreen to finish what the barn started. Don't bloody tempt me, Devan. Don't you bloody dare!"

Retreating to Peace

"You wouldn't," he said, letting out a breath that had sat tightly in his chest. Devan tugged at his seat belt and shuffled his foot in the foot well. There were pins and needles in his one good leg, and he wasn't stamping his feet as though a belligerent child who wanted to go faster.

"As much as you want to, to speed up and slam the breaks on, Aditi," he had found an itch and he wanted to scratch at it. "You wouldn't want to send me to my death. You have picked me up, you are driving me-albeit slowly-home," he arched a brow, and met her eyes in the rear-view mirror. "You might have huffed, puffed, rolled your eyes when I spoke to the nurses, but you also gave me your hand. You put your hand into mine and got me to my feet. Plus you were bricking it entirely, cold hands and trembling, Aditi." He saw her eyes dilate and then flick back to the road. "I've never felt your hands shake so much. I don't think for one moment, that you would let me strop and sulk in St. Vincent's. You sulk all you want," said Devan, slapping his hands onto his thighs. "But bloody well put your foot down. Take me home, tear a strip off me, smack me down and send me to Kingdom come. Change gear and frickin' well sod the speed limit." His tone had risen well above the sound of mangled music on the radio. "Do as you wish, I will not complain," he said snatching his eyes from the mirror.

It was a good thing he did, as he was forced to hold onto his seat as Aditi crunched at the cars gears. She then put her foot down, blowing away any cobwebs that might have formed in the engine.

Chapter 21

How they got back to Oakview without being stopped by Dray Palmer the sheriff who lived in the area was something of a miracle. Devan had been expecting his parents to be happily ensconced at the B&B. However, his illusions were smashed to smithereens when his mother hurriedly tumbled out of Great Aunt Claudie as he and Aditi pulled up. As he clambered out with his crutches, Devan was almost knocked down as he was swamped by his mother's arms. She made no apologies for smothering him in kisses as she cried.

"Let the boy breathe would you, Avni," his father tapped at his son's shoulders to release him; only to land the biggest hug that he could muster around Devan's shoulders. "Don't be a jackass," he uttered into his ear. "You sent your mother and me to hell and back. Don't you dare break Aditi, Devan. If you know what is good for you, you keep her. Sod that boyfriend of hers. Be the bigger man, do you hear me, young man?" Richard pulled aside and rubbed away the lipstick residue that his wife had left upon Devan's cheeks.

Having listened to the edict, Devan nodded and forced a smile onto his face. He then did his best to hobble along as his parents decided to escort him into the house. Apparently, they had been overseeing the furnishing and fitting whilst he had been gone. He stopped short of the house, and rested his elbow on a crutch. Aditi had hung back a little from the family. For a good few minutes, they eyeballed one another. Holding out his hand, Devan hoped that she would take it.

"Come on," said Avni, stepping forward and nudging Aditi. "You'll need to help him keep up, get him up the stairs. All being well, Devan won't be a hop-a-long forever."

Aditi had looked straight through him; he had never felt the harsh, heavy bore of her eyes or for it to land so coldly upon him.

It would be the first week of October before Devan was brave enough to venture into the Brewer's barn. September had swirled passed, turned him on his heel and allowed him to be a little mobile. His leg was healing rather quickly, and of that he was glad. His parents had remained in town, and Devan was a little less glad of this. Having extended their stay, this allowed Avni to fuss over him and ensure that he did little beyond putting his foot up. With this, he had spent time and lots of it, looking sideways at the barn and plotting revenge. The stupid thing had broken his bones, but it wouldn't have his spirit.

Aditi had also remained. Any mention of her leaving was always kyboshed sharply by his parents. They would eventually fly away and be home for Christmas. It was over dinners and breakfast that they aired their unsolicited wishes. If Aditi had nothing better to alongside looking for charities that might need a lawyer, she could look after their boy. He was too far away from them for regular visits; with Aditi here, they had good faith in Devan recovering quickly and effectively.

There had been a video call not too long after Devan had come home. He had very conveniently eavesdropped from outside the second bedroom that Aditi had claimed for her own. His parents had claimed the third and whilst they were here, there would be separate his and hers bedrooms. This might have been his roof, but his parents still managed to pervade Peace with their rules. Rules that they had broken themselves nearly forty years ago, but there was no way, no how that their precious son would repeat their mistake.

In the call, Aditi had finally spoken with Chris and ended what she defiantly labelled as a poor excuse for an adult relationship. Devan had rather enjoyed hearing it all pan out.

"Enough is enough," Aditi had said, her bottom lip trembling and pulling him closer to the door. He could see her, as he peered through the gap between the door and the frame. Her big, beautiful, shining, eyes were starting to sparkle with tears. "Devan, I would run half way across the world for; Devan, I would watch all over night, just to make sure that he woke up-I did that-and I'd do it again. You, Chris, I wouldn't do that for you," Aditi's lips turned into a snarling grimace. "You, Chris, have stalled, skulked, scoffed at everything that I have suggested that we do. It was always a pain, an 'I suppose so', 'if you want to' and 'if I have to'. Not once, did you say yes, okay and why not? I tried, tried to wait. I was ready and always, for you to step up. I would have claimed you for my own; but no," she shook her head, and her long, dark, silken tresses shimmered in the light of the lamp by her bed. "I'm done and with this poor excuse for an adult relationship. Devan claimed me, and you, Christopher Feltham can go bloody whistle."

Devan had almost fallen through the door as he heard his name and Aditi slammed her laptop closed.

She had thrown it aside and then flown towards him at the door through which he was tumbling. Rather than ending up on the floor, he had fallen straight into her arms.

"All right, missis, I've got you," Devan's words were half mangled as they tumbled out of his mouth and he were caught by Aditi.

"No, sunshine, I've got *you*," laughed Aditi, trying not to fall over and holding her feet firmly onto the floor. Her toes were bright pink, and he noticed that they were in need of clipping. "Please don't fall over," she said, using her size ten frame to prop him and support him. "You might break another chuffing leg, and I'm not doing that whole nursey thing again. No so flipping soon, anyway."

"But you would, again?" he asked, setting his own stripy sock clad foot more firmly onto the ground. "Having been claimed," added Devan, freeing a hand and waving it towards the laptop. "Is this an adult relationship then, Aditi, and a proper one?" he couldn't help but give a throating laugh. "You might have to show me if it is," Devan surreptitiously looked over his shoulder to check if he could hear his parents rattle around. "That would mean doing all sorts of adult stuff, you know. Oh, and for the record; you claimed me," he grinned like the cat who had got the cream as he pressed his nose against hers.

"They went out ages ago," Aditi said throwing her eyes behind. "I can show you, all the adult stuff. That's not a problem." Pulling him into her room, she kicked the door closed behind them.

Things had changed; dramatically.

There was still something else to conquer and to claim. Devan took his time walking to the barn. He had long since dispensed with his crutched but still had to wear a brace around his leg to support damaged muscles that were still healing. Physiotherapy kept him reasonably mobile. He was fed up of being shoved into a corner by his parents and Aditi as the last of the furnishing was completed. Devan was doing his best to recover so that he might be rid of two of the three other adults. The third member of the trio, he wanted to keep; Devan wanted to keep Aditi close and for as long as physically possible.

Going to the barn was all part of the plan. Just like he had all those month ago, he pushed open the door; this time had to flick on a light. As the strip light flickered on and flooded the building, Devan saw that it was all a little different from the last time. The roof had been fixed, the floor too. Exposed brickwork had been patched up, and the whole thing didn't look so haggard and decrepit. Even all the rusty machinery had been removed; he remembered something that his father had told him, and how his mother had gone on something of a cleaning rampage. She believed the barn was a death trap, but had rather saved him a job of tidying things.

Part hobbling, part shuffling, Devan travelled to the center of the barn so that he might survey it all. Tilting his head back, he saw the mezzanine over hang. Falling through it, he had caused a hole long since repaired. There was no evidence whatsoever and with his near fatal brush with gravity. The barn was big, just under a third of the size of the house. There was enough room to swing a cat, may be a couple of cats. He would be able to host a party in here of fifty people just fine. What he couldn't remember and for the life of him, was how he managed to meet and greet that many people whilst he had been here. There was Dray, Dexie, Kiki and Laura to name a few. Then there was the Peace town council that he hoped to play onside. If they were invited to this, they may agree to some other plans he wanted to get off the drawing board. Fifty people would fit, and in his barn.

In his head, Devan imagined seating and a canopy, with all sorts of celebratory decorations festooned all over the rafters. He paced up and down, stretching out his strides to measure the space. "Chairs," he said out loud, threading his hands through his locks and feeling his temples pulse. "God, I hope that we can get them all in. Crap, what if it snows?!" he shouted, his words bounced out and were vibrated as they echoed back at him.

"Oi!" There was sharp whistle that followed, smacking him straight between the shoulder blades. "You really should see your face," giggled Aditi as she closed the door behind her and walked into the barn. "And what are you doing with your hands, pulling your hair out already?" she asked, tutting. "You walked off in a huff and Avni got a bit worried. Said that you were acting shifty and have been for days," Aditi arched a manicured brow and stood directly in front of him. "I know why, you know why. You might want to tell them, Devan and before they send in the clowns or the men in white coats, for that matter." Taking a step forward, she hooked a finger into a belt hook of his jeans. "Once my parents get here, there will be questions and by the dozen. There will be lots, especially when the priest from Colorado rocks up. Not to mention the celebrant person that you've booked for the legalities."

"He confirmed?" he drew down his arms and placed his hands on her hips. "We need all that licensing stuff, the rubella thing."

"On the list for tomorrow," she replied. "I've got the fifty-three dollars, identity stuff and even your inside leg. Look, this going to be fine," Aditi moved her hands and pressed them to his stubbly jaw. "Remind me again, how we got this far? I forget."

Taking her hands from his face and into his, Devan held her palms. "You mentioned something about an adult relationship," he replied. "I said that adults generally fall in love, get married and have babies. You asked me if I wanted to," he continued as he looked down and traced his fingers along the lines etched by fate on her palms. "Took me half an hour to think about it whilst you were in the shower; I said all right then, how about an October wedding. Jesus, I've never seen you pull a face like that or smack me so hard when you thought I was pratting around. Still a bit sore actually," he said pulling a hand away and rubbing his hip.

With her hands free, Aditi grasped at his red t-shirt and elbowed poked him in the stomach. "So if anyone asked," she queried, "Who proposed to whom?"

"You," Devan replied. "You were the one that asked about the adult relationship," he added, returning his hands to her hips. "I went along with it, provided that we have a no frills, no fuss, backyard wedding."

"No fuss!" Aditi shrieked, her voice hitting the rafters. "You're having two ceremonies; a Hindu sacrament one, the other ecumenical. Both under this roof!" she said raising a maroon tipped finger to the ceiling. "This is one hell of a shotgun, even for cowboy country. A quick I do and down at the town hall really wasn't going to cut it."

Leaning forward, Devan kissed the end of Aditi's nose. "But where's the drama in that; that would have been boring," he said softly, finding her lips and meaning it. "You and I are anything but boring," he said surfacing after a while. "Might be in Montana, but I don't think we're cut out for jam making."

"Nope," agreed Aditi, draping her arms around his neck. "Especially as I have to fly back home two days later. Six months of sabbatical is over; and way over six months."

Devan felt the moment go pop; a heaviness swung like a lead in his stomach. "We'll make this work. Don't ask me how," he said kissing her nose again. "But we will."

"I hope so," said Aditi, threading her fingers below his shirt. "Adult relationship and all that."

Chapter 22

Both sets of parents were notified and exactly forty-eight hours before; they were somewhat stunned into silence.

"Scrap your plans for Halloween," Devan had said over dinner as he placed a bowlful of salad leaves at the table. "Aditi plans to save my soul, make an honest man of me and marry me in the barn," he added, taking his seat and unfolding a beige napkin. "That's Tuesday," he said looking at his parents who had been holding their cutlery.

Aditi's parents span their heads towards her.

"I'm getting married," nodded Devan and towards Aditi. "Bon appetite."

As two families about to be joined, they all spent the next two days sprucing up the farmhouse and the barn. Chairs were moved into the barn, there was a sound system rigged up and Aditi had also found a band that could play on short notice. On the day itself, there would be two ceremonies. Devan had spent hours studying the religious one, with videos and asking his mum all sorts of questions. Having spent years avoiding his ethnic and spiritual roots, he now didn't have long to find them and to embrace them. These roots were however important to Aditi; she in turn was important and to him.

The first ceremony would be conducted by the priest drafted in from Colorado but had no legal rooting. Hence the need for a second one; it would be an ecumenical and firmly very legal ceremony that would be recognized by the state and beyond. Oakview was prepped and readied for one hell of a shindig with enough food and drink for a small cotillion.

When the day finally came, Devan awoke with the dawn and didn't need singing birds to herald the day's proceedings. There were no twittering birds that day, what triggered him was the flood of almost white light that filled his room having filtered through the curtains. Sliding out of bed and pulling aside one of the curtains, Devan peered the window. "Oh, great! Absolutely fricking marvelous," he huffed, closing the curtains and thundering towards his bedside table. Picking up his 'phone, he tapped the screen to make a call.

"Go away," came the not so pleasant greeting as the call connected.

"Look outside," said Devan, marching back to the window. His heart throbbed with his footfall across the carpet.

"Sod off, Devan," said Aditi. "I don't need your drama and today."

He could hear her moving and over the line. Devan waited, and waited to hear what she would say for about a minute and a half.

"Crap, it snowed," Aditi pronounced loudly.

So loudly, that he almost recoiled back and dropped his 'phone. He could hear across the line and through the walls. Aditi was quite literally the girl next door today.

"It's okay," continued Aditi. "It's only snow. Maybe I can borrow wellingtons…."

"Only snow," Devan collapsed onto his bed. "This is not British snow, Aditi; British snow melts and goes away. This is Peace snow, Montana Snow; snow that bloody well hurts people."

"Oh grow up," groaned Aditi. "Hell, high water and bloody snow will not stop us and today. Since you are up, why not stick the kettle on, eh?" And with that, Aditi hung up.

He was left looking at his 'phone whilst in his boxers. Throwing the device aside, he got up and got dressed. Devan had four hours and to clear a path between the barn and the house. But first, he needed tea. He would have to stick the kettle on. Aditi was yet to marry him, but was bang on the money when it came to having a morning brew.

Sheer determination spurred Devan to dig away snow to form a path with neat piles either side. He had an hour and a half before things kicked off, heading into the house he had to eat, shower and change. All of this was done without colliding with Aditi. Somehow, over the last two days, they had managed to avoid each other. With two sets of parents in the house, some rules were still being enforced even though the whole process of nuptials was deviating from the norm. Guests would be arriving soon and there were signs posted all the way from the gates directing them down the drive and to the barn.

The Coultrie and Rao seniors were tasked with ticking things off lists, directing caterers and managing the running of the day. They were occupied so as not to derail the bride and groom. All Devan could think about was turning up on time whilst hoping that Aditi did the same.

At ten o'clock, Devan knocked on Aditi's door and waited. Taking in long breath that felt like ice across his teeth, he adjusted the black bow tie at his collar. His nerves were starting to shred and he smoothed down his crisp, white dress shirt and removed a sprig of lint that had somehow landed upon his cummerbund.

"Hold on, two seconds!" Aditi's voice was muffled behind the door and he could hear things being thrown about.

"What, why?" he asked, panic rising in his gut.

"—werries," came the reply as the door swung open and Aditi appeared before him.

Pursing his lips together, Devan blew out his cheeks. Aditi Rao stood before him dressed in the brightest of vermillion. Foregoing a traditional sari or lengha, she wore a floor length rockabilly cocktail dress with a sweetheart neckline. He followed the cut of the bodice, where yards of crinoline flowed from her nipped in waist. Aditi's shoulders were covered and with a fluffy white stole dotted with crystals. Then he heard and saw the red and white glass bangles that jangled at her wrists; wrists that, like her hands, were intricately tattooed with patterns made in henna. Devan couldn't utter a single word as she lifted her dress to reveal a pair of shiny, red, very new looking, wellington boots.

"I checked the weather forecast about a week ago," she said beaming. "I was not going to wear heels in snow that hurts people. Are you ready? Only I would really like to marry you today and twice."

Devan didn't need asking twice as he took Aditi by the hand and whisked her down the stairs; her skirts and petticoats bustle between them as they moved. He wanted to marry this woman, in her bright red wellingtons, and as soon as possible.

"Don't run so quick," yelled Aditi, trying to hold her dress above grass. She wasn't resisting as she was pulled along the path that he had cleared and toward the barn.

Once outside, Devan rapped on the door to alert the gathered guests of their arrival.

"Ready?" he asked, breathless and able to hear his heart thudding in his chest. He held her hand still, and tightly; he couldn't let go, he would never let go. Her hand was cold and trembling. The stole really wasn't enough for outside.

"Ready," nodded Aditi.

"You claimed me," he whispered, his bottom lip was starting to quiver. Still holding onto her hand, he pressed his free hand to the door. "I ran and I retreated to Peace; I thought it was all over for me. It wasn't the end though, Aditi, it was just the start."

As the door swung open, those gathered in the barn rose to welcome the bride and group with applause. Applause that sounded almost thunderous as it rose to the rafters. Devan couldn't hear it or see the guests. His eyes were fixed on Aditi as they headed towards the celebrant standing in the center of the barn and beneath a vermillion, raw silk canopy.

Devan had retreated to Peace and in pieces of the emotional kind. He had been claimed by Aditi, and now he could love, heal and perhaps be whole again. As for jam making in Montana, maybe and one day.

About the author

Punam Farmah is a teacher of Psychology and Social Sciences with horticultural tendencies, a trained listener, and lives in Birmingham, England. Her allotment is a short distance away, and forms the field for the natural experiments documented in this book. She is very appreciative of the help from the rest of her family and acknowledges that without them, this book would be devoid of any words, motivation or happy thoughts. When not teaching or experimenting with the plot, she rather likes Star Trek, Shakespeare, the Whedon-verse as well as seeing what can be made with the preserving pan.

To follow along with all of her adventures:
www.horticulturalhobbit.com
www.twitter.com/horticulturalh
Also on Facebook:
Search for Petal: Horticultural 'Obbit
Other works:
Playing with Plant Pots: Tales from the allotment
Sow, Grow and Eat: From plot to kitchen
Fragments

Peace Continues with
Peace and Comfort by Jeanetta Sneed

Kayley White wants to start a new life, one where nobody knows her or her daughter, Chelsea. The small town of Peace, Montana offers exactly what she needs and more - the perfect opportunity to follow her dream of owning a veterinary clinic. When Carter Armstrong comes knocking at her door, she's more than blessed to have help stretching her tight budget.

Unfortunately, Carter is exactly the kind of man she should avoid, and Kayley refuses to get involved with him on any other level. But as long days turn into even longer nights, the two spend increasingly more time together. While they make her dreams a reality, Carter begins to grow on her.

Is Kayley's resolve strong enough to stay away from him, or will she eventually give in?

You can find more details about Peace at:
www.peacenovellaseries.com/
Facebook.com/PeaceSeriesNovella

Previously released Peace novellas:
Songs of Peace
Love in Peace
What Peace Remains
Reclaiming Peace
Seeking Peace
A Haven in Peace
Peace and Harmony
The Philosophy of Peace

Coming soon from Peace:
Peace and Comfort
Peace in Flames
Peace, Love and Misunderstanding
A Dusty Road to Peace
Peace in the Storm
Summer of Peace
Peace of Me
Peace Out

Printed in Great Britain
by Amazon